SEASON OF DANGER

Grid Down Survival Series, Book 6

Judith A. Barrett

SEASON OF DANGER

GRID DOWN SURVIVAL, BOOK 6

Published in the United States of America by Wobbly Creek, LLC

2022 Georgia

wobblycreek.com

Cover by Wobbly Creek, LLC

ISBN 978-1-953-87033-9

DEDICATION

SEASON OF DANGER is dedicated to children everywhere, the magic of snow, and to the joy that the December holidays bring.

PREVIOUSLY. . .

STUART

The grid has been down for several years; it's been hard because in addition to electrical power, the economy, government, law enforcement, and everything we'd taken for granted collapsed with one exception: family and friends.

Probably the best decision Aimee Louise, Rosalie, and I made was to come to my dad's farm in Georgia. We expected a short visit to help him out, but when the murdering gangs swept Florida, we stayed; Major, who is Angel and Red's grandfather, fled Florida with his wife; Mr. Young, an elderly neighbor; my former boss, Sheriff Jack Starr, his wife, Molly, and their children.

I've known since the first day I gazed into her blue eyes that I would marry Angel; she is the smartest and the most talented girl I've ever known. I was happy to wait until she finally came around to my way of thinking. Actually, I take back what I said: the best decision Angel and I made was to be married at my folks' farm.

RED aka ROSALIE

Besides the fact that people say Angel is autistic, and those who know her think she's brilliant, I have something else to add. We have eight families in the four farmhouses that are in close proximity of each other with a total of eleven children in addition to dogs, chickens, goats, and cows. I've got a list, if you need it. Angel's original name was Aimee Louise, but we all call her Angel now, except six-year-old Henry: he calls her Mama Angel because she and Stuart have kind of adopted him.

Stuart left off the most important detail of all: we had a double wedding, and my Andy and I were married at the Newtons' farm too. I have so much more to tell you about Andy, who is absolutely dreamy; Angel wants me to wrap it up, but first I should probably mention her clouds.

Angel can't see facial expressions and says it's the autism; instead, she sees clouds that kind of hang over people's heads or maybe they obscure their faces. Who knows? I can't explain it, but the clouds reveal a person's true feelings and nature. She's saved us more than once when she spotted what she calls a danger cloud.

CHAPTER ONE

Angel and Red raced down the stairs, and Red grinned as she and Angel dashed into the kitchen. "We just heard the most exciting news on the ham radio this morning; we weren't sure if it was important to keep it a secret."

Stuart's mom, Sandra, brushed back her graying hair that had fallen over her eyes when she pulled out the biscuits from the oven. She straightened her back and smiled at the two young women. "I need a haircut, but that's no secret. What's your news?" she asked.

Stuart's dad, Scott, rose from the dining table, drained his coffee cup, and snatched two biscuits from the pan. "Ouch, hot. I'll leave you all to your secrets."

After Scott grabbed his jacket, Henry's lab, Brody, and Brandon's lab, Tracker, rushed outside with him.

Red brushed her untamable red hair away from her face and tugged at the bottom of her sweatshirt as she glanced down the hallway then whispered, "Christmas is next week."

"Seriously? Christmas is actually next week? I've lost track. Have I missed any birthdays?"

"Aunt Molly keeps track of the birthdays," Angel said.

"That's right." Sandra fanned her face with a potholder.

"We heard it on the ham radio, so it must be true," Red said.

Sandra asked, "Did you just bite your lip, Red? You always bite your lip when you've said something that's not completely accurate. What's the secret? That it's Christmas, or who said it on the radio?"

Red giggled. "Angel told me it wouldn't take long for you to figure it out."

Sandra flipped the biscuits upside down onto a plate then turned on the gas burner to heat water for Angel's tea.

"All I know is that Christmas is next week." Sandra grinned as she put another pan of biscuits in the oven. "It's cold enough, and Farmer Blanche told me yesterday that her old bones told her it's going to snow. Of course, I told her that wasn't possible because we live in Georgia."

Blanche came into the kitchen; she wore her favorite overalls and a red and black plaid flannel shirt. "And what did I tell you, Missy?"

Sandra snorted. "You told me I was an old fuddy-duddy and needed to believe snow is possible, even in southern Georgia."

Blanche nodded. "Well then, next week is Christmas, and we'll have snow. Do we get to pick which day?"

"Are all the children outside?" Louisa asked as she came into the kitchen and poured herself a cup of coffee then held it with two hands. She wore a turquoise turtleneck that was complemented by her dark skin. "It was never this cold in south Florida, and it's definitely too cold out there for me. Why are we picking a day? My favorite day is Thursday because both Mandy and Jimmy were born on a Thursday, and Thursday's child has far to go."

"What a coincidence," Sandra said. "It's Thursday, isn't it?"

"Yes, Thursday." Red elbowed Angel.

Angel quietly left the kitchen then slipped up the stairs.

"I'm just going to mosey on outside for a breath of fresh air," Blanche headed toward the back door.

"Oh no, you won't, you old sneak," Sandra growled. "It's all or none."

The three women grabbed their coats and had a minor collision in the rush to be first out the door.

"Age before beauty," Blanche cackled as she tried to close the door behind her.

Louisa caught the door, then she and Sandra pushed past Blanche and hurried outside.

When Angel returned and sat with Red at the table, she whispered, "Mr. Young said Thursday is good for them too."

"Truthfully, it's too cold out there for a foot race." Blanche returned to the stove to pour herself a cup of coffee. She joined Angel and Red and sipped her coffee. "What gave you the idea of celebrating Christmas? Are we going full bore?"

"The works," Angel said. "I learned that from Henry."

"We're talking Santa Claus, Christmas dinner, presents, Secret Santas, a decorated tree, a turkey, a goose, or whatever our hunters can harvest," Red said.

"Dibs on the decorations," Blanche said.

"They're yours, but in the spirit of the season, you might want to share," Red said.

Blanche snorted then flounced out of the kitchen with her coffee cup in her hand. "I planned to share the entire time."

"That walk of Blanche's was a classic example of what Henry would call busted." Red giggled.

"It's more fun when you add your interpretations," Angel said.

The back door flew open, and Henry, eight-year-old Brandon, and Louisa's six-year-old son, Jimmy, burst inside. Angel covered her ears as they squealed, and Blanche hurried to the kitchen as Sandra, Louisa, and Mandy followed the boys inside.

Jimmy shouted, "Mom told us Christmas is in five days, and we have to get ready. Farmer Blanche, Mom said you were our Christmas expert and had everything under control. What's our plan? What are we going to do first? Are we going to get presents?" Jimmy hung his head as he asked softly, "From, you know, Santa?"

Ten-year-old Mandy sniffed at her brother.

"Funny you should ask, Jimmy; let's go into the living room, and I'll tell you a story after I grab a bit more chuckwagon coffee."

Red put her arm around Mandy. "There's a big advantage to being a little kid at Christmas, which is exactly what Angel and I plan to do."

"You and Angel? I can be a little kid too, right?" Mandy stared at Red.

"Of course, you can."

Mandy followed the boys.

"Sorry to break our pact, Sandra, but I can't pass up a Farmer Blanche story, especially one about Christmas." Before Louisa left the kitchen, she whispered, "I'll tell you the story later."

"Do we need to go to Major's farm to tell the rest of our families about the upcoming holiday?" Sandra asked.

"Angel told Mr. Young on the radio," Red said.

Sandra asked, "What is it that Molly always says? 'This family is a well-oiled...'" Sandra was interrupted by a loud crash from the living room. "Except when we aren't," Sandra continued.

"Do you want me to see what happened?" Red asked.

"No, Farmer Blanche will have it all cleaned up and the evidence well-hidden by the time you get in there. I learned that lesson not long after Cal and Blanche moved in with us. She covers for her buckaroos." Sandra chuckled.

Scott came inside. "I'm going to save the rest of my outdoor chores for this afternoon when it's warmer; Stuart, Andy, and David will be in soon. Why is everyone smiling?"

"Christmas is next week," Red said.

"Christmas is exactly what we need after our two recent deaths: Peyton, then Jennie died the next day after suffering from cancer so long. We've all been down since Peyton and Jennie died," Sandra said. "We'll always miss Peyton, but I know she'd agree that the children, and the rest of us too, need Christmas."

"Is a big holiday celebration going to be too much for David and Brandon? Peyton was your best friend, Sandra, but to lose a wife and mother..." Scott's voice trailed off.

"We kind of talked to David last night; you know, just general what if stuff," Red said.

"David agreed with you, Mom." Angel said.

"Well, that sneaky polecat. David didn't say a thing this morning," Scott headed toward his coat.

"Don't run off," Sandra said. "I'll finish frying bacon then scramble a big mess of eggs, if you'll make pancakes. I already mixed up your batter for you."

"What about the biscuits?" Scott asked.

"I was planning on biscuit and ham sandwiches for midmorning snack or lunch."

Red cut off a large piece of smoked ham, then she sliced ham while Angel assembled the sandwiches. Red nibbled on the last bit of the salty ham. After they finished, Sandra said, "You two are fast."

"I need a platter for the pancakes," Scott said.

"Did someone say pancakes?" Doc Larkin asked as he and Noel, Mandy and Jimmy's dad, came into the kitchen. Angel poured their coffee, and Red set the table.

When Farmer Blanche, Louisa, and all the children came into the kitchen, Brandon said, "Wow. Papa Scott's making pancakes."

"I assume everyone has made their bed and picked up their clothes in their room," Sandra said.

When the children raced upstairs, Sandra called out, "Wash your hands before you come to the table."

"You live for that, don't you, honey?" Scott asked.

"Sure do; it never gets old," Sandra said.

"Can I check my room later?" Doc Larkin said. "I'm too old to run to make my bed."

Noel smirked. "I'm still recuperating, so I shouldn't run because we don't want me to relapse."

"You two get a pass, just this once." Sandra waved her wooden spoon at them then smiled as she turned her attention back to the eggs on the stove.

After Doc Larkin and Noel sat at the table, Mandy hurried down the stairs.

"Daddy, next Thursday is Christmas, and I'm a kid." Mandy beamed.

"I think I might be a kid too if next Thursday is Christmas," Noel said. "Do you think that's okay?"

Mandy nodded. "Being a kid at Christmas is the best."

While the children, the two men, Louisa, and Farmer Blanche ate, Red asked, "Shall we round up the men from outside?"

"Good idea," Sandra said.

When Angel and Red joined Stuart, Andy, David, and Cal in the barn, Red said, "Pancakes are on the griddle, and we're cleared for Christmas next Thursday."

"Christmas is next Thursday?" Cal narrowed his eyes at the other men. "Was I the only one who wasn't in on that?"

"You talk in your sleep," David said. "We had to come up with something to lift everyone's spirits, but Angel's idea of Christmas was the best, and we needed a few details ironed out first."

"Is it even December?" Cal asked.

"Of course." Red snorted. "It couldn't be practically Christmas if it wasn't December."

"Blanche said it will snow for Christmas," Angel added.

"I'm sold; if my wife says it's going to snow in south Georgia next week, then it must be Christmas. I suspect Sandra and Blanche will take charge of all the details, and the rest of us will wait for our orders."

"Exactly," Angel said.

"Did you have any doubts?" Stuart chuckled.

On their way to the farmhouse, Red said, "One more thing: Mandy has agreed that Christmas is for kids, so she, Angel, and I are kids."

"You are too, honey," Angel said as Stuart put his arm around her shoulders while they walked.

"Is there a test I can study for?" Andy asked.

"You'll always be a kid." Red giggled as Andy swaggered to the house.

David chuckled. "Peyton always said I was an overgrown kid, so I'm covered too."

When they reached the house, Cal said, "I'm married to a kid, so I must be a kid too."

Red went to the living room to join the children while everyone else sat at the table for pancakes.

When Andy stared at Red as she left, Sandra said, "Red sliced the ham for me; I suspect she may have filled up on ham for her breakfast."

After breakfast, Angel and Louisa cleared the table while Stuart and Andy washed dishes and pans.

"I'd like to go to Major's and talk to Molly about Christmas. What's your schedule, Blanche? Could you go with me?" Sandra asked.

"My morning's yours," Blanche said. "I'll have my rifle and my pistol."

"I need Noel to train me on a rifle; I'll leave my shotgun, but I'll have my sidearm," Sandra said.

"Angel, could you drive them in the utility vehicle that Red named 48-4?" Scott asked.

"Certainly."

"As tempting as that is, we don't need to use our precious supply of gas just to go to Major's for a chat with Molly, and I need to walk off a few pounds anyway," Sandra said. "Is that okay with you, Blanche?"

"I'd much rather walk, and we can plan on our way there."

Scott wrapped his arms around Sandra's ample waist. "Don't walk off too much because you're perfect the way you are."

"Oh, you," Sandra tittered as she lightly smacked his arm.

"I'll let Mr. Young know they're going to have two visitors." Angel dashed upstairs to the radio then returned.

"All set," she said.

After Sandra and Blanche left, Angel slipped her handheld radio into her belt as Red said, "Let's all go for a run."

"Me too?" Andy asked. "You leave me when we go running."

Red raised her eyebrows, and Andy shrugged. When Angel followed them, Stuart followed her.

Red and Angel led the way as they trotted around the house, and David joined the four of them as they ran along the path to the Smith barn that was between the Newton farm and the Webster farm, owned by Andy's uncle, Leo.

When they reached the Smith barn, David said, "You never ask Andy to run with you and Angel, Red. Something's up."

"He's right." Stuart crossed his arms. "Does the militia need us?"

"The militia is holding their own, but there's a part of a gang from Atlanta that learned there was a doctor in south Georgia and is on their way to kidnap him," Red said.

"We're certain they are coming for Phil's son," Angel said.

"Doc Scooter is still at Major's farm," David said quietly.

"We didn't want to postpone Christmas because everyone needs it, but Mr. Young will suggest that Major's farm and the farm next to them, the Cabellos', have Christmas together, and we have Christmas with Leo," Angel said.

"I have a little more information about Leo," David said. "Cal has been an intermediary for Mr. Young and has been talking to Leo about opening his home to Doc Scooter, his family, and his parents. Leo admitted the only reason he didn't want anyone staying at his house was because Jennie was so ill and couldn't tolerate any noise at all. As long as he has his radio room with the door he can close if the household becomes too noisy, Cal thinks it would work."

"I'd worry less about Uncle Leo if there was another family with him, and if Doc Scooter is at Leo's, we can defend the house. Do we put a push on that, so it happens before Christmas?" Andy asked.

David exhaled. "I don't think we should."

"We'll take direction from the experts," Stuart said, "but at least we'll be ready."

"I'll check our transport trucks to be sure they all start. I've needed to do a little maintenance on them for a while. I know Cal will help me, then we'll gas up one of them for a move," David said.

"Leo knows about Christmas and the gang headed this way," Angel said. "I want to talk to him."

"Now?" Stuart asked.

"Yes."

"We'll go too," Red said.

"No one travels alone. Go back with David, so he can talk to Cal, then you and Andy can run to Leo's, but don't leave Andy behind," Angel said.

"You've gotten really bossy, Mrs. Newton," Red grumbled.

David chuckled.

* * *

Angel ran alongside Stuart, so he could set the pace. "Why are we going to talk to Leo?" he asked.

"His equipment is better than mine, and so is his antenna. He may have more information about the gang, and I'd like to understand how amicable he actually is to Doc Scooter, his family, Phil, and Deana moving in with him. Maybe it's something that could happen tomorrow or at the latest, the day after that. One good thing is that the gang will be looking for Doc Grayson."

"Who's Doc Grayson?"

"Scooter's name is Grayson; they called him Doc Grayson in Atlanta."

"How do you know all these things?"

"I pay attention to details, but you knew that," Angel said.

"Doc Scooter doesn't seem like a very professional name. Should we switch to Doc Grayson?"

"No, because that's who the gang is looking for."

"Right; you just told me that." Stuart chuckled. "I amaze myself with how quick I am sometimes, and that's sarcasm."

"Maybe we should drop the doc part," Angel said.

Stuart nodded. "I'll mention it to Scooter to see what he says."

When they reached the house, Angel clicked the squelch on her radio twice then knocked twice on the door and went inside.

"Why did you knock then go right in?" Stuart whispered.

"It's our code."

"Hey, Angel. Come on back," Leo called out.

Stuart hung back, so Angel could talk to Leo alone.

"Are you here about the splinter group from that large gang in Atlanta?" Leo pulled off his headset then inserted an earbud.

"Yes, your radio is better than mine. I heard they were coming to south Georgia to kidnap an ER doctor, but I don't know when to expect them or if they are likely to come here."

"I think they are headed here because the last I heard, they were headed toward the interstate and then will continue toward the Alabama state line. My guess is that they would be here in no more than three days."

"Do you know who they are looking for?" she asked.

"I heard Doc Grayson on the radio."

"Did you know Doc Grayson is Scooter?"

"Are you certain? Of course, you are." Leo exhaled. "Cal, Mr. Young, and I have been talking about my old friend, Phil, and Phil's son, Scooter, moving here to give some relief at the Cabellos' house. There are a passel of kids at the Cabellos' as it is; Phil's family would be better off here, and it would be easier for you and your team to defend them." Leo sighed. "Jennie always loved a good fight. I'm sorry she'll miss out."

Angel examined his cloud. *Tinges of sadness but mostly a strong sense of duty to serve. Interesting.*

"Are you ready for an invasion of small children and a bossy woman? Phil's wife Deana won't let you skip meals or not bathe," Angel said.

"I'll deal with it. How quickly can we move them here?" Leo asked.

"We're checking the transport trucks, so we can move them in only one trip; if we have a truck ready, we could move them tomorrow if they can pack that quickly. I suspect they unpacked only the necessities for the families because the Cabellos' house was full before they showed up."

"They could move in today, as far as I'm concerned. There's plenty of room. There are no sheets on any of the beds, and I haven't cleaned in ages, so I think Deana will be kept busy for a while. I'll enjoy having Phil around; he's a long-time ham like me, and maybe we can come up with more ways to boost the signal here."

Angel rose. "I'll see how fast I can get everyone moving."

Before she reached the door, Leo said, "Thanks, Angel. I needed a chance to talk it out but come back anytime I can help."

Angel almost bumped into Stuart, who was lurking in the hall outside the radio room.

After they were outside, he said, "I heard everything. I love how you operate."

"What do we do next?"

"Check in with Dad then decide who goes with us to tell Phil and Scooter they can move anytime."

On their way back to the Newton farm, they met Red and Andy.

"That was fast. Did Uncle Leo refuse to talk to you?" Andy asked.

"Let's get back to the house, so we can tell you and Dad at the same time," Stuart said.

Angel and Red took off at their fastest pace. "We'll meet you in the barn," Red called out.

* * *

When Stuart and Andy reached the barn, Stuart smiled. *Another Angel and Red argument.*

He shook his head. *You'd think Red would learn.*

"You might as well tell me what Leo told you; after all, Stuart told Andy on the way here, and you know it," Red said.

"No, he didn't because they would have run as fast as they could and wouldn't have time to talk."

"Why? Just because it's logical? You don't know how fast they ran," Red snapped.

When Stuart and Andy walked into the barn, Scott was smiling as he leaned against the back wall. He winked at Stuart.

Andy strolled to the fiery Red and when he put his arm around her, Red leaned against him and smiled.

"Leo said Phil and his family could move into his house any time," Angel said.

"You went straight to the punchline," Red growled. "I wanted to hear the whole story."

Stuart smiled. "It was beautiful. Angel asked Leo if he was ready for an invasion of small children and a bossy woman, Deana, and Leo asked how quickly we could move them. David and Cal are checking the transport trucks and will have one ready to go to the Cabellos' house."

"David and Cal? How did they get involved so quickly?" Scott asked.

"When Red invited the three of us to go for a run, David tagged along because he said he knew something was up. Red never invites me to run with her and Angel because those two don't know how to slow down when they run together," Andy said.

Stuart stepped closer to Angel, and she leaned against him. "Angel asked Leo what he'd heard on his radio because it has a better range than ours does." Stuart shook his head. "I thought she was just trying to warm him up by talking about radios first, but I was wrong."

"We've heard a faction of a powerful gang based in Atlanta is headed toward south Georgia to kidnap an ER doctor for their front lines. Leo said they were looking for Doc Grayson from Atlanta and are headed toward us. Leo thought they'd be here in less than three days," Angel said.

Scott frowned. "What am I missing?"

"Scooter was Phil's son's nickname when he was a kid; he was called by his given name, Grayson, at the hospital in Atlanta," Stuart said.

"Sandra's going to ask me, so I need to know: wouldn't we be better off bringing Scooter's wife and children here?" Scott asked.

"I don't think that's our choice, Dad, but we can offer; I think you and I should go to the Cabellos' to talk to Phil and Scooter," Stuart said.

Red narrowed her eyes. "Why can't..."

Stuart interrupted Red. "We're short four shooters; if Dad and I leave, we'll be short six. We can't empty the house."

Red glared at him; Andy elbowed Red. "Logical."

Red giggled. "It's all around us, isn't it?"

"Let's go inside and tell Noel, Louisa, and Doc Larkin what we're going to do," Scott said.

"David and Cal need to know too," Angel said.

Red gazed at Andy, and he said, "Go ahead; I'll stay here."

As Angel and Red dashed out the barn door toward the shortcut to the Smith barn, Andy said, "I can talk to the folks in the house about what's going on while you get ready to leave, and I'll alert Mr. Young on the radio."

"Do you want to take 48-4, Dad?" Stuart asked after they gathered their rifles and were headed outside.

"No, I'll be fine as long as I don't have to run with Angel and Red."

Stuart snorted. "It took me forever to work up to running fast enough to keep them in sight. I still can't keep up when the two of them run together."

Scott jogged, and Stuart trotted along beside him on their long driveway. When they reached the road, they stopped to check the road then continued to the Cabellos' driveway.

"It's a lot smoother and a little easier to run on the pavement because the uneven gravel threw me off balance." Scott picked up his pace.

After they reached the Cabellos' driveway, Scott said, "It always surprises me how close this is to Major's driveway. I don't think I paid much attention to it until Major and his family moved here."

When they approached the house, Phil and Major were waiting for them near the driveway.

"Sheriff, I mean Jack, and I came to tell Phil you were on your way here, and we stayed because we're nosy," Major shook his head. "I'm still having trouble remembering to call him Jack. Do you want to go inside?"

"No, let's talk first," Stuart said as Jack joined them at the driveway, then Nate Cabello came out of the house and stood near the trees.

"Phil, Leo has invited you, Scooter, and your families to move into his house with him anytime," Scott said.

"Who cracked open the old coot's calcified mind?" Phil asked.

"Angel," Stuart said.

"That's my Angel." Phil laughed. "She's a miracle worker, isn't she?"

Stuart nodded. "Did you hear about the gang coming this way because they wanted to find the doctor from Atlanta?"

CHAPTER TWO

Major frowned. "We knew they were looking for a doctor they'd heard was in south Georgia or North Florida, but we didn't know they were headed west."

"Leo heard they were looking for a Doctor Grayson from Atlanta," Scott said.

Phil's face tightened. "That's Scooter. How far away are they?"

"Leo estimates no more than three days."

Nate left then returned with Scooter.

"I don't get it; why would they come all this way for a doctor?" Jack asked.

"I wouldn't think there would be any doctors left in Atlanta since the collapse and the rioting. It's not unusual for a disgruntled lieutenant in a gang to pull away a few followers, especially as the gang grows in numbers and geographically. This could be a faction that was familiar with the hospital and has been looking for doctors, so they can be independent of the larger gang," Major said.

"That's along my line of thinking, Major, especially since they were in Atlanta and headed south to find Doctor Grayson," Stuart said.

"Maybe they'll go to our hometown," Phil said.

Nate shook his head. "Everybody knows your hometown was overrun, and I'll bet everyone who took off when you did knew that you headed northwest."

Phil nodded. "Everybody knew about Angel, and a lot of people would have known that we would have tried to find Major."

"I'd be willing to be the optimist and say they'll never find their way here, but the realist in me says that we should prepare, just in case," Scott said.

"I've been thinking about Leo's offer, and it would ease a lot of day-to-day pressure on all the families at the Cabellos' if we moved to Leo's farm," Phil said.

"I agree, Dad," Scooter said. "How soon can Leo be ready for us? It will take us only a few hours to pack up, but it will take us quite a while to move because we have so much stuff put away in the barn."

"Leo said any time. We have a heavy-duty transport truck that we can load here then unload at Leo's," Stuart said.

"What about Christmas?"

When all the men stared at Nate, he shrugged. "Some of us have priorities."

"Christmas is still Christmas. We may consider not trying to pull everyone together at one house, but we might want to plan on our closest farms getting together on Christmas Eve or Christmas Day for the children," Scott said.

"Do we want to slow down that high-powered Christmas planning session going on at our house?" Major asked.

Scott sighed. "Yes, I'll leave Stuart here to work out the logistics for the move and go right now."

"I'll back you up," Jack said. "That's a rough crowd over there."

Scott nodded as he followed Jack to the shortcut. "Tell me about it."

"Show me what's in the barn, so I can see if we'd need a second truck," Stuart said.

"Follow me," Scooter said.

Major accompanied them to the barn.

On the way, Stuart said, "I don't know how much of the conversation you caught, but Leo told us there is a gang from Atlanta that is looking for Doc Grayson from Atlanta."

Scooter's face tightened. "No, I didn't hear that. Does anyone know why?"

"Not really; we hoped you might," Stuart said.

"We'll talk later. What about the transport truck, Major?" Scooter asked.

"One of the transport trucks will be fine."

"So what's our plan?" Scooter asked as Phil joined them at the barn.

"We can bring the truck here in the morning and load it then take the truck to Leo's. Do you have enough fuel to follow us? It would be ideal if we could move the truck and all of y'all in one trip."

"I've got enough gas in my truck to make it," Phil said. "Worst case is we all pile into my pickup."

"Are you a runner, Scooter?" Stuart asked.

"Sure am."

"Our runners can easily run from here to Leo's farm," Stuart said.

"My wife is a runner too; we'd be fine with running, and the kids would love riding in the truck with Grandma and Grandpa," Scooter said. "I'd like to talk to my wife, though, before you leave."

"Go right ahead; we may be here a while," Stuart said.

"I didn't want to say anything in front of Scooter," Phil said as he and Stuart strolled back to the house, "but have there been any thoughts about the children if we are attacked?"

"One option we've considered is that Scooter's children could come to my parents' farm. We were attacked not long ago and have some good defense barriers in place, but we never came up with a defensive strategy for Leo's house, and I'm not sure that three days is enough time to put anything in place. Another option is we have a sizeable group of excellent marksmen, and we would be close enough to assist you before or even after an attack begins. Red, for example, is stellar. We named her Dead Eye Red long ago, and she's only improved."

"Thank you, we have four shooters, and all of us are good shots, but the children will require close supervision, which leaves us with three."

After everyone else went into the house, Stuart waited in the driveway for Scott.

Scott came through the shortcut. "I told Deana, Molly, Sandra, and Blanche about the plan to move Deana's family to Leo's and about our idea of two houses joining together for Christmas rather than coordinating one big celebration, and all of them loved the idea. Sandra told me I was brilliant, then she and Blanche left, and they will get with Deana after the move. What do you think about the timing?"

"Scooter asked me to hang around until he talked to his wife, so we'll see."

Scooter came out of the house. "Joyce has already started packing, so we'll be ready when the truck shows up in the morning," He waved then went inside.

"Sounds like we're scheduled for an early morning start."

As they jogged together back to the farm, Stuart asked, "Are we making a mistake moving Phil and his family to Leo's when we have an army headed our way to kidnap Scooter?"

"I expected the four women to jump down my throat for disrupting their plans for Christmas, but I was the hero of the day. I suspect things have been tense at the Cabello house, and Molly must have been worried about them because she hugged me and told me I was awesome then gave me a small box to give to Sandra. When I was walking back from Major's, I realized that an overcrowded house, especially one with five small children and a pregnant woman, would be difficult to defend."

"You're right, Dad. I'll put my energy into moving Phil, getting ready for Christmas, working with David to come up with fortifying Leo's house, and keeping Angel happy."

"Can't think of anything you've left out, Stuart."

Sandra met them at the back door before they made it inside. "When will Deana move to Leo's?" she asked.

"Tomorrow," Scott said.

"Good; come inside and have some Christmas cookies that Louisa and the children made."

Stuart stared at the cookies with the carefully piped Christmas trees with red dots and the cookies that had a green or red smear of frosting on them, and several green- or red-smeared cookies that had a small star cut out in the middle then the small star cookies that had white sprinkles on them.

"Now that's art," Stuart said.

Henry, Brandon, and Jimmy sat at the table while they ate smeared cookies and drank milk; Mandy bit off the top of a Christmas tree then carefully wiped her fingers onto her napkin. All three boys had green and red frosting on their hands and faces.

Sandra, Blanche, and Louisa went into the living room, and Andy came downstairs.

"I've been listening on the ham radio, but there hasn't been anything. Ready to find Angel and Red?"

"Let's go."

When Andy and Stuart reached the trucks, Angel and Red sat on a tailgate, Cal sat on a stump, and David was standing near the truck.

"When do we move Phil and his family?" Red asked.

"First thing tomorrow morning," Stuart said.

"We have two trucks ready to go," Cal said.

"That's great; it looks like we'll only need one, but it's great to have a second one, just in case," Stuart said.

"I want to take the bush hog to Leo's driveway, so we can drive down it to unload," David said.

"Better yet, remember our alternate driveway? Why don't you clear one wide enough for the truck on the far west side of Leo's property?"

"I like it; I'll do that."

"Do you think you could get the tractor through the shortcut?"

"I might need to take a chainsaw to a couple trees, but yes," David said. "I like your idea; less disturbance to our driveways."

After David and Cal left, Angel said, "We were talking while we waited."

"First thing: I never remember anyone calling Doc Scooter anything besides Scooter, so it seems, as embarrassing it is for me to say, logical that no one in Phil's hometown would know his given name. He's Scooter in south Georgia, and Doc Grayson in Atlanta," Red said.

Stuart nodded. "That's right; I hadn't thought of it either, so if the gang continues asking where Doctor Grayson is, nobody will know who they are talking about. So, how did you know his name was Grayson, Angel?"

"Phil had a framed copy of Scooter's bachelor of science degree on his wall."

"So is it possible that some people did but more likely that they've forgotten?" Stuart asked.

"Only a slight possibility because people don't remember names and rarely remember names that they read years ago, except for Angel," Andy said. "So, what's your conclusion, honey?"

"He's Scooter in south Georgia and Doctor Grayson in Atlanta," Red said. "Y'all need to catch up."

"While we're waiting for David, I want to let Leo know he can plan on Phil's family in the morning," Angel said.

"I'd like to go back to the house, so Cal won't have to stay with David when he takes the tractor through the shortcut," Andy said.

"Let's go," Red said.

"At my pace?" Andy asked.

"If you insist."

On the way to Leo's farm, Stuart said, "I know you're always one step ahead of me. What are you thinking?"

"I'd like any information about the group that Leo can gather," Angel said.

"Do you know what you're going to do with it after you get it?"

"Yes."

Stuart peered at Angel then ran faster to keep up with her. When they reached Leo's house, he said, "Would it be better if I didn't join you in the radio room, so you and Leo can speak freely?"

"Yes."

When Angel opened the door, Leo called out, "More news, Angel? Come on in."

Stuart stood outside of the partially closed door and listened.

"Give me a second to insert this earbud, Angel," Leo said. "Okay, whatcha got?"

"We'll load Phil and Scooter's packed boxes in the morning, then Phil will follow the transport truck to your house. David is clearing a strip for the vehicles to use near the west fence. We have old brush and snags we can throw down to block it after we're finished."

"Jennie has a nice store of food in the pantry and the utility room. Phil is welcome to whatever they can use," Leo said.

"I'm sure they have quite a bit too, but you can let Deana know after they arrive, so she doesn't worry about keeping the food separate."

"I was thinking back to the days before Jennie was sick: she and I ate breakfast together, and she made me lunch and a hot supper. I'm happy to return to regular meals; Jennie always said I was a terrible cook, and she wasn't wrong." Leo chuckled. "What else do you have for me?"

"I need more information about the gang headed our way; for example, I'd like an estimate of the size of the group, and any other information you can gather, like do they have a support vehicle or are they plundering as they go for food, do they have handheld radios, what is their direction of travel and speed, and are they pitching tents or sleeping in the open?"

"This is spy stuff; I love it. I'll have something for you in the morning, Angel."

Stuart smiled at the sound of Leo rubbing his hands together.

"I know you will; I'll see you then."

Stuart stood back from the door, and Angel entered the hallway. After they were outside, Stuart said, "Leo was excited, and I loved your ideas. What are we going to do with what Leo finds out for you?"

"We have several possibilities; it depends on the information."

On their way back to the Newton farm, Stuart asked, "What's our plan for this afternoon, or have we already done everything this morning?"

"Was that sarcasm?" Angel asked.

"No, I was wondering because it seems like there is nothing left to do until tomorrow."

"After David and Andy are available, we have to check Leo's farmhouse for defense the same way we did Dad's house then decide what we can do in the next two days."

Stuart snorted. "I wish I had said it was sarcasm because I can't believe I forgot about Leo's farmhouse."

"It's why we're a team," Angel said.

Stuart stopped on the path, and Angel immediately stopped too. He grinned and hugged her then leaned down for a passionate kiss.

When he ended their kiss with a light peck on her open lips, he said, "Yep, still a team."

They strolled back toward the Smith barn with their arms around each other.

"I'm sorry for how rough the times are, but I'm glad we're together," he said.

As they neared the Smith barn, they heard the roar of the tractor as it headed their way on the path. Andy carried his rifle as he trotted along behind David. David waved then continued past the barn and toward the shortcut to Leo's farm.

"I have ham biscuits, cookies, and water for our lunches in my backpack. Red didn't want to come because she said the tractor is too stinky." Andy ran to catch up with David.

"Stinky tractor sounds like an excuse to me," Stuart said before they resumed their run. "I think Red's up to something, but I'm not going to ask you what's going on because even though I'm sure you know, it must be a secret."

When Angel began running, Stuart mumbled, "I was right."

He pushed to catch up with her.

After they reached the house, Stuart said, "I'm going to check in with Dad at the barn. I'll be in soon."

"I'll come with you, unless it's a secret."

Stuart chuckled. "Come on, let's see what he's come up with."

As they strolled into the barn, Brody and Tracker rushed to greet them; Angel rubbed Brody's ears, and Stuart scratched Tracker's.

Scott said, "You're just in time. Cal and I have been talking about our defense and Leo's. Cal and I plan to go to Leo's after lunch."

"Okay if we go with you, Dad?" Angel asked.

"I'd appreciate it. As far as our house, I'm still concerned about the blind spot on our east side; I'm not sure what we can do, but we need to look at it again."

"I wouldn't mind sending David, Andy, and Blanche to Leo's after we get back; they're all highly skilled in different areas of defense and will have unique perspectives," Cal said.

"I need to check on lunch," Scott said.

Angel and Stuart followed Scott and Cal to the house. On the way, Angel nudged Stuart with her shoulder, then he nudged her back. Angel giggled, and Stuart chuckled as they continued to nudge each other on the way to the house.

Before they went inside, Stuart hugged her and whispered, "On top of everything else, you're fun."

Stuart bumped into Scott who stood in the doorway, then Angel bumped into Stuart.

"Come on in," Blanche said. "Don't be shy; it's only glitter."

Stuart stared at the scattered glitter, pieces of colored paper, glue, paper glued together, tape, and crayons.

"Aunt Molly sent us Christmas crafts, Dad," Henry said. "Isn't it neat?"

"Not sure I'd use the term 'neat' for this particular project," Scott whispered as he stepped back and closer to Angel, and she cleared her throat.

"Aunt Molly has everything, doesn't she? Are you making decorations?" Stuart asked.

"Sure are. Designer Blanche told us we'll need decorations for our tree," Mandy said.

"I'm making a star using cones. It's very tricky," Brandon said.

"It looks hard, but you are doing very well," Angel said.

"I like Christmas," Jimmy said.

Henry nodded, "I do too."

"Lunch is al fresco, if that's what you're looking for," Blanche said. "We have the table reserved until suppertime. We ate lunch before we started our projects, and Mama Sandra said we could have a snack after we finish our projects and clean up."

Sandra came into the kitchen. "Here's the platter of ham biscuits. If you eat them all, we'll make more, so help yourself. There's coffee on the stove, and the water in the kettle is hot, Angel, if you care for a cup of tea. Louisa and I are eating in the living room because it was too chilly for us outside; you're welcome to join us. I think Red's on the radio."

"Go ahead and get your food, honey; I'd like to check the radio to hear what's going on," Angel said.

When Angel hurried into her bedroom, which doubled as the radio room, Red motioned for her to take the headset.

Angel listened then smiled. "Leo's stirring up a little trouble, isn't he? Sounds like he started up a cantankerous conversation, and people are correcting him. He's collecting a lot of information in a short amount of time. I'll have to remember that technique."

Red nodded and her bubbly, dancing cloud sparkled.

Red asked, "What did my cloud do?"

"Did you smile? It suddenly developed sparkles." Angel handed Red the headset. "Do you want some lunch? I'll bring you a ham biscuit and a glass of water."

"That would be fine. The salty ham tastes really good."

"When are you going to tell him?" Angel asked..

"Tell who?" Red growled as she put on the headset and turned her back on Angel.

Angel rushed to the door and bumped into Stuart. She raced downstairs and Stuart followed her then waited while she took a ham biscuit and a glass of water to Red. When she returned, he asked, "Inside or outside?"

"Outside."

While they sat at the bench near the garden, Stuart asked, "What's going on?"

Angel took a bite of her ham biscuit.

"Tell me if I'm wrong: Red's pregnant."

Angel took another bite.

"I won't say anything." Stuart ate the last bite of his ham biscuit then exhaled.

"Do you want to see if Dad and Cal are ready to go?" Angel asked.

"Is that okay? You haven't finished eating."

"I can eat on the way."

"You're the best." Stuart kissed her, then they hurried to the house as Scott and Cal came out of the back door.

"Grab your backpack; we're ready to go," Scott said.

Angel put on her sweatshirt, then she and Stuart picked up their rifles.

"What's up?" Red asked. "Shouldn't I be going too?"

Stuart slipped out the door while Angel said, "We're going to check out Leo's house for security. You may want to wait and go with Andy and David when they do a security assessment."

Red nodded. "I think I will."

"You need to tell him because he thinks something is wrong."

Red slammed her hand on the table. "How do you know? Does he know? Were you and Stuart discussing it? Did Stuart tell you Andy thinks something is wrong?"

Red glared at Angel then exhaled and sat at the table. "I'm sometimes a little hot-headed, but lately I have a super-short fuse. Of course, you wouldn't have told Stuart. Andy's cloud told you." Red's chuckle was hollow. "He's even asked me if I'm okay at least five times today alone. I haven't told him because he'll want to tell everyone, and I don't know why that's a problem. I'll tell him then ask him why I'm worried; I'll bet he'll know; he's really smart."

"Yes, he is."

Angel dashed out the back door then joined Stuart at the short-cut.

"Is everything okay?" he asked as they ran to catch up with Scott and Cal.

"Is now," she said.

"We'll talk later," Stuart said.

* * *

"When Stuart and Angel catch up with us, will we have to run with them, or will they breeze on by?" Cal asked as he and Scott strode along the path at a steady, fast pace.

Scott chuckled. "Can you imagine how much pain we'd have for the next two weeks if we tried to run with them?"

"I brought a pad and pen; I'd like to do a sketch of the house and the location of windows," Cal said.

"That's a great idea; it will give the entire team good reference points."

When Stuart and Angel raced past them, Cal said, "They came up so fast behind us that I didn't even hear them; they've obviously broken the sound barrier."

Scott nodded. "I've been thinking about how we can pull Leo then Phil and Scooter into planning for their security. I suspect Phil has some experience, but I'm not sure about Leo, and I have no clue about Scooter."

"I think you've hit on the key fault with our rush to design their security. We should be the support team and stand aside, so the experts at Leo's house can tell us what they need," Cal said. "So, how do we slow down our hotshots?"

"I know my answer is always Angel; let's tell her our concern then turn it over to her," Scott said.

"As the support team, we'll need an inventory of the guns and ammunition in the house," Cal said. "I'll talk to Leo, but I'm certain he'd rather you and I did it for him; he probably keeps a pistol and maybe a rifle in his radio room, but all the rest of the guns and ammo were Jennie's."

"I hadn't thought about it, but it's definitely critical information, and I'm sure Leo has no idea what is there; do you want to talk to him alone?" Scott asked. "According to Stuart, Angel talks to Leo alone while Stuart waits in the hallway."

"Well, there you are: we'll ask Angel to talk to him," Cal said. "Let's take a breather."

Scott stopped and gazed at the swaying treetops in the woods around them. "I'll take the subtle approach and talk to Stuart; Angel will let us know when we can get started."

"Good thing we don't walk too fast," Cal said. "Sometimes we need to do a few circles on the skating rink before we come to the answer."

Scott chuckled. "Getting ready for our snow?"

"Might as well." Cal shrugged. "Don't tell her I said so, but I've never known Blanche to be wrong in all our years of marriage."

When they reached the Smith barn, Stuart and Angel weren't there, so they continued on to Leo's farm then joined the young couple on the driveway and listened to the roar of the tractor on the far edge of Leo's property.

"David's making good time, isn't he?" Scott cleared his throat. "Cal and I were talking on our way over here. Cal can make a good sketch of the outside of the house with the windows and doors, so we'll have a quick idea of potential blind spots. We don't want Leo to feel like we're steamrolling him, though, with our security ideas. I can talk to Phil and Scooter tomorrow morning; they have a vested interest in the security of the home. I'll let them know we're definitely available to assist and support them."

"Jennie's guns," Angel said.

Stuart nodded. "We should talk to Andy."

"Andy may not know; I need to talk to Leo." Angel headed toward the house, and Stuart followed her.

Cal stared as the two went into the house. "That was amazing; your approach was so subtle that I completely missed the part where you mentioned Jennifer's guns."

"So did I." Scott chuckled. "I keep forgetting how brilliant Angel is. Now I wonder how long she's been planning to talk to Leo about Jennie and was waiting for the right time."

CHAPTER THREE

When Angel and Stuart went inside the house, Leo called out, "Glad you're here, Angel. Did Stuart come inside with you? He'll want to hear this too."

After Angel and Stuart went into the radio room, Angel sat on the visitor's chair that Leo had added to his radio room specifically for her; Stuart stood in the doorway, so he could watch the back door from the hallway.

"One of the hams spotted a large gang on a state road at sunset, and they have two support vehicles. They are well-organized because about half of the group from what he could see were lined up for an evening meal at the truck while most of the others unloaded and set up large canopies off the road, and a small group stood guard. His best estimate was there were about fifty to sixty men. He purposely didn't give their location because it would have pinpointed his, but he's a regular and located south of Macon."

"That limits their travel time and makes them more vulnerable between sunset and sunrise," Angel said.

"I'm glad you stopped by because I had news for you, but there must have been something on your mind," Leo said.

"Jennie's guns."

"Jennie told me years ago she had an inventory sheet of her guns, but I'm not sure where it is, and it's certain to be out of date. I do have keys to her four gun safes in my drawer here. I hadn't thought of it earlier, but there may be ammunition and guns in some of the closets, especially in the bedrooms and maybe in the kitchen. Do you and Stuart have time to do a good search?"

"We could do that; Cal and Dad are checking the path from Dad's house to here, so we'll have to let them know we'll be here for a while," Angel said.

"Ask them if they could help you, then you could take your time and be as thorough as possible. We need the house to be as safe as possible for the babies," Leo said.

"I agree; we'll be right back," Angel said.

After they joined Scott and Cal, Stuart recounted the conversation between Angel and Leo.

"Leo definitely nailed the real reason we should check for Jennie's guns, didn't he?" Cal shook his head as the four of them went into the house.

"We'll start with the unlocked guns and ammo first," Stuart said. "Bring whatever you find to the kitchen; after we've finished our search, we can talk to Leo, but I suspect he will say that what's not secured needs to be removed from the house. Angel and I will take the upstairs."

After they were upstairs, Stuart said, "Let's do one room at a time together." He glanced around. "I'd forgotten how big their house is; there are four bedrooms and two bathrooms up here."

They started with the master bedroom. "Jennie kept her guns in top shape," Stuart said. "That's really amazing considering how sick she was the last few months of her life."

After they had cleared the closets, drawers, and under the bed, Stuart said, "Now comes the hard work: carrying all this downstairs. Why don't I work on that while you start on the next bedroom?"

After an hour of steady work, Stuart and Angel carried down the last of the guns and ammo that they found upstairs.

"We need someone to look behind us," Stuart said. "After Andy and David return, I'll ask Andy to see if we missed anything."

Scott and Cal came inside the house.

"I told Leo we'd found quite a few and offered to take them out of the house, and he agreed," Cal said.

"We've been using the utility cart to haul what we found to the closest truck. It might not be the best place for permanent storage, but it's at least out of the house. After we have everything in the back of the truck, we can see what we have and go from there," Scott said.

"I'll ask Noel for his suggestions for safe storage; as a gun shop owner, he may have some ideas we wouldn't have considered," Cal said.

"We didn't check the radio room, Angel, because we thought Leo would be more comfortable if you and Stuart did that. We'll carry out what you brought down from upstairs."

Angel clicked on her handheld twice and knocked on the kitchen table, then she and Stuart went to Leo's room.

"All done?" Leo asked.

"Everywhere except your radio room," Angel said.

"I don't think you'll find anything except my pistol I keep in my drawer and the rifle in the corner."

Angel started in the closet and found two small boxes filled with ammo.

When she showed the boxes to Leo, he said, "This ammo isn't for my gun or the rifle. Guess you better do a thorough check."

After they finished, Leo said, "When people were leaving the area, they'd ask Jennie if she'd keep their ammo that they didn't have room to take with them. No one wanted to leave ammo or guns for any scavengers. I guess Jennie became the local armory."

Stuart chuckled. "That's what it looks like to me; I think it's great that Jennie gave so many people peace of mind."

Leo gave Angel a keyring with four keys. "I have no idea which key fits which safe, but at least there are only four. All the safes are upstairs, but I guess you know that since you've spent the last hour or so up there."

When Angel and Stuart reached the top of the stairs, Angel said, "The tractor stopped at the road; something's wrong."

She dashed down the stairs and raced outside the house, and Stuart followed her. She gave the keyring to Scott. "These are the keys to the safes upstairs. We need to inventory them."

"We'll take care of it," Scott said.

Angel and Stuart raced up the driveway toward the road. When they were close to the road, Angel stopped, so Stuart did too.

"I hear two men with Andy and David, but there could be more," she whispered.

She led the way through the high grass and trees parallel to the road until they neared the far west side of Leo's property then crouched and listened again.

She whispered, "The men have a young boy they are using as a hostage. They just told Andy to drop his rifle; Andy's trying to stall."

Angel stayed low and crept toward the voices, and Stuart quietly followed.

Stuart heard the man growl, "Drop it now."

When the two men came into sight, one man held a gun to the head of a pale, painfully thin boy, about thirteen years old, with dark blond hair that hung to his shoulders. The man had twisted the neck of the boy's stained and torn T-shirt at the back with his other hand.

"Can I put on the safety first?" Andy asked.

The boy wiggled to loosen the T-shirt across his throat. "I can't breathe; it's too tight, man."

Stuart knelt on one knee in the grass as he aimed at the man and waited for an open shot.

"Shut up, kid." The man twisted the boy's collar tighter, and the man lost his grip on the boy's shirt as the boy slumped and fell to the ground. The second man laughed and aimed his rifle at Andy, and the first man aimed his gun at the boy.

When the two shots rang out almost simultaneously, the two men dropped, and the boy jumped away from them then raced across the road to the ditch on the other side.

"Where are you two?" Andy looked around.

Stuart and Angel walked toward Andy and David.

"Where's Red? I heard two shots at once."

Stuart rolled his eyes. "Remember who taught Red to shoot? Major taught Angel at the same time."

"I didn't even have time to grab my rifle," David growled. "They appeared out of nowhere."

"I wish I could cover my ears when I shoot." Angel grumbled before she jumped the ditch then raced across the road.

When Angel reached the ditch on the other side of the road, she disappeared into the woods then reappeared with a twenty-two rifle and a knapsack; the young boy carried a younger girl about four years old on his back, piggy-back style; she had black hair, light brown skin, and a tear-stained face with dark, sunken eyes.

The girl clutched the boy's T-shirt with her grimy fists and leaned her head against his back; she was even more emaciated than he was, and her thread-bare shirt, shorts, and sockless feet in shoes that threatened to fall off were no match for the weather.

"My name is Ethan; I don't know what her name is. She's been too scared to talk. I found her in the woods a couple of days ago. I was trying to find something for her to eat when these two ambushed me not far from here. They dragged me here, so they could get more rifles, or something. I have no idea how she followed us; she must have crawled through the woods and dragged along my rifle and bag." Ethan shook his head. "I was surprised to find her so close."

"Do you think she'd let me carry her?" Stuart asked.

"I don't think so, Mister."

"I'll get 48-4 and come get you." Angel raced back to Leo's farm.

"I'll go with her, if I can catch up." Andy ran after her.

"We found a small blackberry patch yesterday. I couldn't stop her eating, but she ate so many blackberries that she threw up. I've carried her most of today."

"I have some water and a biscuit. I can give you some water and half the biscuit. Do you think I could try to give her some water?"

Ethan nodded.

Stuart handed Ethan a cup of water. "Take small sips."

While Ethan gulped then took a breath and sipped the water, he stared at Stuart. "Are you a cop?"

"Would it be okay if I am?" Stuart said.

"Yes."

"That's good because I am."

"So am I," David said. "You might be more comfortable if you sit next to the tractor; it makes a good wind break, and I have a jacket we can put over her."

Stuart broke half a biscuit in half then gave it to Ethen. Ethen took a small bite then watched while Stuart poured a little water into the cup and held it close to the little girl. She looked at Ethan, and he nodded. She reached for the cup, and Stuart helped her sip.

After Stuart broke off a small piece of biscuit, he put it in his palm then offered it to her. She snatched it off his hand, shoved it into her mouth, and swallowed it without chewing.

Stuart's heart ached at the sight of her mournful gaze as she searched his face then reached for more biscuit, but Stuart said, "A little more water first. Let's help that biscuit settle in your stomach."

When Stuart smiled and glanced at her cup then her face as he held the cup a little closer to her, she took the cup in both hands and sipped a little more water. After she took her third sip, Stuart pinched off another small piece of biscuit then held out his hand with the biscuit on his palm. She watched Stuart's face as she grabbed the piece of bread and shoved it into her mouth. Stuart mimed chewing, and she copied him, and he smiled. "Good girl."

She nodded.

Ethan said, "You got a way with kids, mister."

"It's what cops do, Ethan; I'm Stuart."

"I'm David, Ethan. How's that biscuit sitting on your stomach?"

"I could handle the other half, Mr. David," Ethan said.

David nodded and gave Ethan the other half of his half biscuit.

Ethan glanced at David. "I've been eating half of what I have and saving the other half for later, then I found her, and I gave her what I could find."

David nodded. "Makes total sense to me; you have good survival instincts and a compassionate heart."

While Ethan broke his biscuit in half, David asked, "Where did you come from?"

After Ethan ate his piece of biscuit, he said, "I've lived with my grandparents, Granny and Pops, on their farm in Alabama since I was a baby. Granny woke me up in the middle of the night and told me to get dressed fast. She opened my bedroom window just enough for me to get out and told me to run away from the house as fast and far as I could. She handed me my rifle and knapsack with some food and ammo then practically shoved me out the window and closed it behind me. I ran into the woods and hid. I heard shouts and gunshots then I saw tall flames in the sky, so I ran away like Granny said. When the sun came up that first morning, I realized I was headed east and didn't see any reason to backtrack. I think that was two weeks ago."

"Was your dad or mom a cop?" David asked as he poured a little more water into Ethan's cup.

Ethan sipped his water. "Granny said my dad was the best cop in the world; she never talked about my mom except once I overheard her tell a friend of hers how tragic it was that my mom died so soon after my dad."

Ethan's eyes widened, and his face drained of all color. "I hear a truck coming our way. We need to hide." He jumped up then clutched at the tractor seat for balance but missed.

David caught him before he fell. "It's okay. That's Angel coming to pick you up in our four by four; she'll take you to our farmhouse, and Mama Sandra will take care of you and sweet girl."

"Is she your mama?" Ethan asked.

David chuckled. "No, she's actually Stuart's mama, but we have four children at the farm house, and we've all gotten into the habit of calling her Mama Sandra because that's what the kids call her."

"I'm twelve; are they any other boys my age there?"

"Not at our house, but there's a boy at Angel's grandfather's farm-house that is nearby; I'm not sure, but I think he may be twelve too."

"What about little girls?" Ethan asked as he glanced at the small girl.

"There are three little girls at Nate's house; he lives close to Angel's grandfather."

The girl's eyes brightened when David said three little girls, and Stuart smiled. "I think all three of them are six."

The little girl's smile was weak as she sipped on her water.

"Their names are Dolly, Sam, and Cami Sue," Stuart continued, and the little girl listened intently.

"Sam and Cami Sue are twins. Dolly has a dog named Pixie and pretty dark brown eyes just like you. Her mama and dad speak English and Spanish. Do you know any Spanish?" Stuart asked.

The little girl glanced at Stuart then gave a quick nod.

"Can I guess your name? Is your name George?"

The little girl glared at Stuart.

"Sorry, I was trying to make a joke because I know there's no way I can guess your name."

The little girl reached out and patted Stuart's hand.

"Thanks," he said.

After Angel pulled up then parked 48-4, she, Red, and Andy hopped out.

The little girl stared at Red.

"Her hair is very red, isn't it?" Stuart whispered, and the little girl nodded.

"Did Mr. Stuart tell you about Dolly?" Red asked as she knelt next to the little girl.

The little girl continued to stare at Red and nodded.

"Your beautiful eyes remind me of Dolly. Are you sassy?" Red asked.

The little girl ducked her head then nodded slightly with the same earlier weak smile.

"Oh, good because I'm sassy too. Do you want to ride next to me to Mama Sandra's farm?" Red asked as she held out her hand.

The little girl quickly looked at Ethan who said, "I'm riding too. I might get to ride in the front with Miss Angel where you can watch me."

The little girl took Red's hand and struggled to rise, so Red swooped her up. Red whispered, "My name is Red. Do you know why?"

The little girl nodded and patted Red's hair as Red carried her to 48-4. Andy spread out the quilt they had brought across the seat, then after Red sat the little girl in the middle of the seat, Red and Andy wrapped the frail child with the quilt. Red sat next to the girl, put her arm around her, and snuggled her. The small child leaned against Red.

"Are you okay?" Red whispered, and the little girl nodded. "I brought snacks. Would you like a little snack?"

The little girl's eyes widened, and she nodded.

Red gave her a small cracker with strawberry jam on it.

David helped Ethan to the front seat, and Andy helped Ethan put on a jacket that was too large but warm.

"All loaded and ready to go," David said.

"Here is a snack for you, Ethan." Red handed him a cracker sandwich: two crackers with strawberry jam in the middle.

Angel turned on the engine then turned around. "Do you want to go fast or slow, Ethan?"

"Fast." He grinned.

As Angel roared to the Newton farm at a moderate speed, Stuart smiled. "Red's always been famous for her snacks."

"Brandon and Henry told me if I ever needed a snack to ask Red; I never knew she was such a softie." Andy chuckled. "What do we do next?"

"We need to find the best place to cross the ditch, so I'll know where to stop, then we're done here, and I can take the tractor back to our house," David said.

"Will you be okay with the tractor if we scout the ditch?" Andy asked.

"Yep."

They crossed the ditch then took turns watching their back as they walked down the road toward Leo's driveway.

They hadn't gone far when Andy said, "There's a culvert that has filled in with debris. I wonder if Uncle Leo knew he had another option for his driveway."

"I don't know, but a driveway straight to the house like he has makes sense to me," Stuart dropped a glove in the road. "We're not likely to miss it, but it doesn't hurt for us to have a visual."

They ran back to the tractor.

"We found a culvert. We can snip the fence then repair it after we move them," Andy said.

"Cal and I can repair the fence. Let's go." David bush-hogged the grass and weeds twenty yards from the fence as he drove parallel to the road.

When Andy spotted Stuart's glove, he raced to it as a marker for David. David made a wide turn away from the road then continued past the road forty feet from the fence. He made another wide turn toward the road then approached the culvert head-on.

"That's slick," Andy said. "I had no idea why you drove away from the culvert, but it makes sense to me. Our alternate driveway will be hidden immediately after we use it."

"Where do we want to snip the fence?" Stuart asked.

"I'm thinking about six inches from the post, so we can splice it back with more wire, but I need to talk to my consultant," David said.

Stuart smiled. "Ranger Blanche."

David nodded then backed up the tractor in the path he made until he could turn toward the new temporary driveway. "I'm ready to go back."

"We'll be right behind you," Andy said.

After they returned to Leo's farm, David and Andy continued to the Newtons' farm.

Stuart knocked twice on the door then opened it. "It's Stuart, but I'm by myself."

"Come on in, Stuart."

"I'd like to check behind us to be sure we didn't miss any stray guns or loose ammunition. Babies are eagle-eyed creatures, I've been told, and find things no one else would see."

Leo chuckled. "Go right ahead. The radio's pretty quiet this time of day, so you won't be disturbing me at all. Let me know if you have any questions."

After Stuart was satisfied the second floor was clear, he went to Leo's ham radio room.

"Upstairs is clear. Did Dad and Cal finish the inventory for all the safes?"

"Sure did. Cal took his notes with him, but the keys are back in this drawer in case you ever need them."

"I can't see when I would, but thank you."

"Is something on your mind? You seem worried."

"What are you hearing about the militia? I feel drawn to join them, but I don't know why."

"I can't tell you why you feel drawn, but I can tell you there is a lot of discussion about another country invading the US. No one has any concrete information: who, when, how, where, and why are complete unknowns, so most of us consider it an unfounded rumor. I do know the militia is terribly understaffed and undersupplied. The men and women are wholeheartedly dedicated, but they need more skilled marksmen and trainers, and they need people who can reclaim the equipment and supplies the cartels and gangs stole from them."

"Does Angel know about the types of people the militia needs?"

"Of course, she hears the same conversations I do."

That's exactly why I'm worried. "It helped to talk, thanks. I'll check the first floor then head back to the farmhouse."

Leo nodded then put on his headset and turned back to his radio.

After he cleared the main floor, Stuart headed to the truck that had all of Jennie's rifles and pistols. He organized them by type of firearm then caliber and inspected each type.

He shook his head. *All of these need to be cleaned and checked for repairs. I wonder if Major could take on another project. Wait, we've got Noel at Dad's; he's not a hundred percent yet as far as doing very much physically, but he could easily teach other people to clean guns while he inspects each one then repairs the ones that can be fixed and retires the ones that can't.* Stuart smirked. *It always helps to talk things out.*

His eyebrows raised when he heard the distinctive sound of 48-4 as it headed toward Leo's farm. *It's coming fast; Angel's driving.*

When Angel parked, Scott climbed out of the passenger's seat, and Cal stepped out from the back seat.

"Angel, you drive like you run: too fast to be believable and with remarkable skill and grace," Cal said.

Stuart put his arm around Angel and whispered, "That was a compliment, sweetheart."

"Thank you, Cal," she said.

"In case you were wondering, we wouldn't let Angel come get you alone, and she wouldn't walk with us here, so we decided you needed us to do something with all the firearms and came in 48-4," Scott said. "So, what do you need us to do?"

"Load all you can onto 48-4, so we can take them to the farmhouse. We'll need to clean and inspect them; I'm hoping Noel can repair any that need to be fixed. I know I can't."

"I knew that," Cal said.

Scott chuckled. "We'll get to work."

"Do you need for us to help?" Stuart asked.

"No, we'll be fine."

"How are Ethan and the little girl doing?"

"The little girl hid behind Red when she saw Brody and Tracker, but those smart puppies wagged their tails and whimpered as they crawled to her; she sat on the floor and put out her arms, and they snuggled on either side of her and grinned when she put her arms around their necks. Mama Sandra and Mandy coaxed the little girl to take a warm bath. Louisa had some child-safe bubble bath, and the little girl loved it. Sandra said the bathwater was filthy, and the child was covered with scratches and bug bites, but Sandra applied ointment on the open wounds and told me she was relieved that none of them were infected. The bath lifted the little girl's spirits; at first she stayed close to Ethan or Red, but now her small circle of trusted people includes Mama Sandra and Mandy," Scott said.

"That's really great news. What about Ethan?"

"Ethan snapped at everybody except David because he had to take a bath too. I don't know how David escaped except David asked Ethan to help him carry in some lumber. When we left, Chef Blanche was sliding the cookies she and the younger boys made into the oven. Ethan may fold and join the cookie tribe." Scott shook his head. "He managed to get on the wrong side of Red."

"It was a sight to behold," Cal said. "Ethan told Sandra he absolutely would not take a bath, and Sandra couldn't make him. Red growled at him with her scary tiger voice and told him she could, and she would. Noel whispered to me that he'd see me later because he was going to take his bath, and I had to leave the room to keep from being scolded for laughing."

"When Red said in the iciest tone I've ever heard, 'Get in the tub now, Bucko,' Blanche and Sandra put their hands on Brandon's, Henry's, and Jimmy's shoulders to keep them from jumping up from their seats at the dining table," Scott said.

Stuart laughed. "Poor Ethan. Girls are scary, especially Red when anyone crosses her."

"He was amply rewarded for his bravery. After his bath, Red gave him two cracker and jam sandwiches and thanked him, and all the boys patted him on the back after Red left the kitchen. He looks like a completely different boy: he has freckles across the bridge of his nose, his hair is blonde, and his smile is like barbecue sauce: it wound up on everyone's face."

Stuart chuckled. "I wish I could have seen that entire episode, but I would have left the kitchen with Noel and Cal."

"Let's go," Angel said, and they raced toward the house.

She's staying two steps ahead of me.

After they reached the farmhouse, Stuart asked, "Were you daring me to catch up with you, so we could run faster?"

"Yes."

As they went inside, Stuart whispered, "Did you see Red and Andy hugging at the garden? Will this help calm Red's scary side?"

"No."

After they were inside, Angel raced up the stairs to check the ham radio.

"Where are all the kids? Is it story time?" Stuart asked.

"Blanche is telling a story in English and Spanish. She decided that she would include learning Spanish in her stories, crafts, and their outside chores. Louisa has joined them to help Blanche. Louisa reminded us that she grew up in south Florida and is fluent in Spanish. Teacher Blanche promised Angel and me private lessons," Sandra said.

"Did you know Blanche spoke Spanish?" Stuart asked. "Although, since it seems Ranger Blanche knows everything, if we ever have a child appear who speaks German, we'd all be learning German, wouldn't we?"

Sandra chuckled. "You need to get out of my kitchen and find something useful to do besides entertain me with your fanciful theories."

"Where's Noel?" he asked.

"Noel and Doc Larkin are in Noel's bedroom probably plotting an invasion of my kitchen."

Stuart smiled as he hurried to Noel's room.

CHAPTER FOUR

When Stuart stood in the doorway, Doc Larkin said, "We were just talking about sleeping arrangements. Is there enough room in the boys' bedroom for four beds, or should we ask David to build two sets of bunkbeds?"

"I'm not sure; I'll check with Mom, but she may have already decided what's going to work."

The two men nodded as Stuart continued, "Noel, Dad and Cal will be on their way here with Jennie's guns and ammo after they load what they can on 48-4. They may need to make two trips."

Noel breathed out a long whistle. "We'll need to clean and inspect them."

"Dad thought you could offer gun cleaning training, then you could inspect them. Angel, Red, and I could help with the inspection, and Angel could probably help you with any repairs."

"Any thoughts on where we can store them?" Doc Larkin asked.

"We'll definitely need to figure that out right away," Noel said.

"In the interim, we can lock them in my closet, or David could even build storage racks in my closet. All my clothes are in the old highboy chest of drawers that Sandra put in there for me; I don't have anything in the closet except my medical supplies, and it wouldn't hurt to have them locked up too," Doc said.

"I think that's ideal because we'd want them inside, locked up, but easily accessible," Noel said. "Where's David? We need him to look at Doc's closet."

"I'll chase him down," Stuart said.

When he returned to the kitchen, Stuart asked, "Mom, do you know where David is?"

"He said something about checking the west side of the house," Sandra said.

Stuart rounded the house and spotted David as he paced off the distance from the house to the trees.

"I'd like to clear some of these trees. I don't like the cover they give to someone who is firing on the house."

Stuart peered at the trees. "How much would you want to take down?"

"I'd be happy with clearing another twenty yards; I know the priority between now and next Wednesday is Leo's house, but this side has been bothering me, and I wanted to measure it. What's going on?"

"We need a place to store Jennie's guns, and Doc Larkin suggested using his closet."

"Let's look at it; we'll want shelves for the pistols and racks for the guns at a minimum."

As they strolled to the house, David asked, "How many guns are there?"

"I sorted them by type of firearm and caliber, but that was earlier this morning, so in my professional opinion, there are lots." Stuart shook his head. "Angel has an inventory sheet. We can look at it to get an idea."

"I'll get a rough idea from the inventory. We may have to use my closet too; I've been reluctant to pack away Peyton's clothes, but maybe Sandra would do that for me."

"She would do it with love," Stuart said.

"You're right; she and Peyton were close friends." David stared at the sky then gulped. "Sorry, I still tear up a bit."

"Mom does too; I know it must be hard," Stuart said as they reached the house.

After they went inside, David continued to Doc Larkin's bedroom, and Stuart took the stairs two at a time then bounded into his and Angel's bedroom that doubled as the radio room.

Angel turned and waved when Stuart came into the room, then she pointed to her headset. He kissed the top of her head then sat next to her and waited.

She removed her headset. "You first."

Stuart smiled. "We need your inventory sheet."

"Come back, and I'll tell you what I heard."

Stuart dashed down the steps and gave the inventory sheet to Noel then returned to join Angel.

"I'm back," Stuart slid into the chair next to Angel.

"I caught a snippet of a conversation from a sporadic e. The operator said 'Old Jitters' was foaming at the mouth because he thought the team he assigned to find Doctor Grayson was sandbagging, so he's sending a second team. What does sandbagging mean?"

"Purposely going slow to impede progress or sabotage an effort. What does sporadic e mean?"

"A signal skip," Angel said.

"Do we know who or what 'Old Jitters' is?" Stuart asked.

"No, that's the first time I've heard anyone say that," Angel said.

"If the radio operator was talking about the team from the gang that is headed this way, then immediately after we stop the first team, we have to be ready for the second one that is right behind it."

"Yes, unless we can turn the two teams against each other."

"How do we do that?" Stuart asked.

"Talk to the experts." Angel picked up the headset.

"We could write it off as not related to us at all except for the reference to Doctor Grayson." Stuart exhaled.

"Yes." Angel put on her headset and turned her attention to the ham radio.

Stuart was deep in thought as he slowly went down the stairs. *How could we turn the two teams against each other?*

He tripped over Brody's tail as he strolled into the kitchen, and Brody grumbled.

"Sorry, boy; I wasn't paying attention where I was going." Stuart knelt down and rubbed Brody's face in apology.

"What's going on?" Scott asked.

"Feel like going for a walk?" Stuart asked.

"Sure." After both men put on their jackets and picked up their rifles, they went outside.

As they strolled toward the back field, Stuart told his dad what Angel had heard. "Angel said we need to turn the two teams against each other."

Scott exhaled. "She might be right. I'll bet she has an idea of what to do, and I might be thinking the same thing, but I don't like it. Who are our experts?"

"Seems like we have a whole house full of experts: Noel, Andy, David, Blanche, and Cal. Maybe we should ask Leo if he's heard anything about Old Jitters. I'll see if Andy or David is available to run with me to Leo's."

"David is working on the racks and shelves for Doc Larkin's closet. Andy's hovering over Red, so that may be a double deal for you; they're on the front porch. Let me know what Leo says."

Stuart strolled to the front porch. Andy had his arm around Red as they sat on the steps together.

"I need to run see Leo," Stuart said.

"You can't go alone; Andy, go with him because I want to listen to the ham radio and talk to Angel," Red said.

Andy and Red went into the house, then Andy returned with his jacket and rifle.

After Stuart and Andy arrived at Leo's farm, Andy asked, "What are we going to ask Uncle Leo?"

"It's about Jitters, but I don't have a quick explanation, so let's go inside."

"Does this Jitters have a medical condition?" Andy asked.

"I don't think he physically has the jitters; I think he gives other people jitters, but Angel was hoping Leo could clarify."

When they went into the radio room, Leo glanced at them as he removed his headset. "What does Angel want to know?"

Stuart chuckled. "You're right that Angel sent me. She caught a snippet of a conversation on a sporadic e. She wants to know if you've heard anything about an Old Jitters."

"Give me a second, and I'll check my notes." Leo opened the spiral notebook that he kept on his desk and flipped back ten or so pages. "Here's where it starts: three weeks ago, a first time ham said, 'he gives me the jitters.' The only reason I noted it is that it was such a random comment because no one had been talking about feeling nervous."

"Who was the speaker?"

"I don't know because he didn't give a call sign, which isn't all that unusual these days. He seemed to be particularly interested in the weather forecast for south Georgia."

Leo flipped a few pages, "A week later, we were talking about possible freeze warnings, and the same guy wanted to know how reliable the forecast was. I jotted it down because it was another unusual, random comment from the same guy, but the next time he said anything on the ham weather group was this past week. He went into a rant about crazy Old Man Jitters. I didn't record all of his diatribe, but he said Jitters was sending a team on a suicide mission to punish them for defecting. When someone asked him what that had to do with weather, he said that Old Man Jitters will find a way to use it against them."

"I'm thinking your radio operator is obsessing over Jitters and is actually the one who is unhinged," Stuart said.

"That was my thought too until a couple of days ago when a new guy came on and asked about the freeze warning in south Georgia. When one of the hams made a joke about taking over for his buddy on vacation, the new guy denied there had been anyone else interested in the south Georgia weather."

"How could he know whether someone else might have been interested earlier if it was his first time in the group?" Andy asked.

"Exactly." Leo grinned. "I learned that from Angel."

On their way back to the Newton farm, Andy asked, "Do we know anything about this Old Jitters? I wish this was all conjecture, but because Angel is in the middle of it, I know it isn't."

When they went into the kitchen, Sandra was popping corn, and Teacher Blanche was telling a story about the origin of snowmen to represent Christmas while the children snacked on popcorn and goat cheese and drank milk.

"When Mama Sandra finishes popping corn for us, I'll show you how to make snow people while Mama Sandra and I prepare supper," Blanche said. "After our craft, we'll follow our bedtime routine. Which is..."

"Bath, snack, bedtime," Brandon, Henry, Jimmy, and Mandy said in unison.

"Bath, snack, bedtime?" Ethan asked. "I've already had a bath today."

"If we wash your scratches and bites and put on fresh antibiotic cream, then you can skip a second bath," Sandra said.

"Okay, I don't want any of my scratches to get infected," Ethan said.

The little girl tugged on Sandra's sleeve, and Sandra said, "You can still enjoy your bubble bath; no change there."

After everyone finished eating supper that evening, Henry snuggled against Angel. "Brandon and I played a game that Mandy taught us to decide who would sleep on the mattress that's on the floor next to Jimmy. It's called rock, paper, scissors. Isn't that a cool name? I won, so I picked the new mattress on the floor because I'm shorter than Brandon. Mama Sandra told us that Rancher Blanche would build us bunkhouse beds, but it might take a day or two before she is done. We're excited about sleeping in the boys' bunkhouse."

"I don't blame you, Henry," Stuart said. "There's nothing better than sleeping in the boys' bunkhouse."

"Dad, you shouldn't say that in front of Mama Angel." Henry frowned and shook his head.

"You are right; I'll apologize to her tonight," Stuart said.

After everyone finished their snack, Mandy whispered to the little girl then said, "Mama Sandra, we're ready to go to bed. She'd like for you to tuck her in and sit with us a while."

"I'd love to," Sandra said.

Sandra carried the lantern as she followed Mandy, who held the little girl's hand, while they went up the stairs to the girls' bedroom.

When Stuart started to follow the boys upstairs, Henry said, "Don't worry, Dad. We'll be fine."

Stuart stared as Ethan followed Henry, Jimmy, and Brandon, who carried their kerosene lantern, upstairs.

Scott put in hand on his son's shoulder. "Take it from an old pro: it's hard when little boys start growing up."

"Is this what it's like, Dad? I'm not really ready for Henry to grow up." Stuart exhaled.

Scott nodded as they headed toward the kitchen.

"After the boys settle, I'll see if I can entice Angel away from the ham radio with a security check," Stuart said.

"Remind her she's got two old men who are on the radio twenty-four hours as her backup."

Stuart chuckled. "I can't do that; she'd take it as a challenge."

After the boys quit talking, and Brandon extinguished their light, Stuart tiptoed upstairs.

When he went into his room, Angel removed her headset, and he whispered, "The boys are in bed and quiet, and Mom is with the girls. Are you ready for our evening security check walk?"

"Just like old times." Angel turned off the radio and extinguished her light, then the two of them slipped quietly down the stairs. After they put on warm jackets and grabbed their rifles, they headed to the back door.

"Wait up," Red said. "Is it security check time? We'll go with you."

The four of them walked around the house in silence as they checked the house and surroundings in the pale moonlight.

When they reached the barn, Andy said, "Red and I would like to talk to you."

After Red sat on one of the steps to the loft, Andy said, "Stuart, Red and I are going to have a baby, and we are excited and scared. Red didn't want to say anything because she's afraid something might happen to the baby."

"Angel told me today she knew because of my cloud, so I talked to Andy," Red said.

"In some cultures, babies aren't even named until they are several months old, so the spirits can't find them and take them away," Angel said.

Red stared at Angel. "I had almost forgotten that Mom told me her granny told her to protect her baby girl from the spirits when she was pregnant by not even whispering her name. When she told Dad, he said he thought she had better sense than to believe an old, senile woman."

Red smiled. "Mom told me her granny was a seer, not senile, and most doctors were smart enough to know that they don't know everything. Dad assumed a girl would be named after his mother, and a boy would be named after his father."

"What was his mother's name?" Stuart asked.

"Rose," Red said, "which is why he always called me Rosie."

Andy chuckled. "Your mom named you Rosalie, so you would have a name that wasn't spoken before you were born. I'm sorry I never met her because she must have been brilliant with a stinging sense of humor."

Red's smile was weak as she nodded.

Andy continued, "We decided to keep any discussion about the baby as low key as possible, but now that we know what's making Red even more nervous, we should definitely avoid talking about names."

"Talk to Mom; she'll help you set the tone, and so will we," Stuart said.

After Angel and Stuart went into their bedroom, Stuart said, "Sweetheart, I owe you an apology."

He held her close as he brushed away her hair from her face and lightly kissed her while he unbuttoned her shirt.

He continued, "Sleeping with you is far more fun than sleeping in a boys' bunkhouse."

* * *

When Stuart woke the next morning, Angel was wrapped in a blanket as she listened to the radio. Stuart leaned in front of her and grinned, and she kissed him.

"Hot tea?" he asked, and she nodded.

He quickly dressed then tiptoed downstairs toward the flickering light in the kitchen.

"I poured your coffee and started Angel's hot tea steeping," Sandra said. "We have two beds in the girls' room, but our younger girl kept sneaking over to Mandy's bed. Mandy told me it was okay with her, so I told her that if the little one flopped around too much, she could shift to the other bed. I told your dad I was worried Mandy would end up on the floor, and he told me if she did, she wouldn't be alone, and I worry too much."

Stuart chuckled and drank his coffee.

"Angel's tea is ready."

Stuart carried the cup of hot tea to the bedroom. He smiled at the flickering light and the folded blanket on the bed. *She waited to dress, so she wouldn't wake me.*

"Here's your tea," he whispered. "I'll let you know when breakfast is ready."

Angel waved as he left the room and quietly closed the door behind him.

After he returned to the kitchen, Sandra refilled his cup.

"Red and Andy talked to me last night when I came downstairs after the two girls were settled," Sandra said. "They are thrilled and terrified, and I understand completely. We decided to keep everything low key and not mention anything to anyone until after Christmas. I'm positive most of the adults have already guessed, but everyone is biding their time and giving Red and Andy time to adjust to the idea. I reminded Red and Andy that Charo and Nate's baby is due anytime, and the new baby will keep everyone busy for a while. I'm making oatmeal this morning because I'm cold."

"Do you want me to start a fire in the fireplace to take off the chill?"

"That would be ideal."

Stuart started the fire, then after it was going strong, he added extra wood   then   returned   to   the kitchen.

"Thanks, Stuart. Speaking of Charo, I asked Angel to tell Mr. Young that we need any of Dolly's or the twins' clothes, shoes, and jackets that they have outgrown for our newest visitor. I found her a nightgown that one of the girls left, but we need fresh clothes and shoes for her today. She can't wear that ripped T-shirt or those shorts that I've already thrown into the rag pile. I need someone to pick up clothes this morning."

"What about Ethan?" Stuart asked.

"I think I have enough of your old clothes for Ethan. I found him pajamas for last night, and clothes that I'm sure will fit."

"I think Nate and Scooter loaded most of the boxes last night; they can bring clothes for the girl this morning."

"Sounds good. Do you want to take Angel's oatmeal upstairs, or will she come downstairs for breakfast?"

"I've already told her I'd let her know when breakfast is ready; if it was up to her, she'd stay glued to the radio all day."

"Oatmeal's going to be ready in a few minutes."

"We need a big meeting this morning after we move Phil and his family to Leo's. I'd like to involve Scooter and Phil in the discussion."

Angel soundlessly raced down the stairs. "We need to pick up the clothes for our girl after all. Mr. Young said the estimated departure time has been delayed because of the size and age of the travelers."

"I guess we'll eat and run," Stuart said.

Sandra nodded. "I'll appreciate having clothes for our little girl. We may have a pair of jeans that fit Henry last year and maybe a shirt, but I think even his pants from last year will swallow her thin frame. What about the ham radio while you're gone?"

"Cal and Red are the most familiar with it, and Blanche or David could jump in except I'd hate to pull them from their projects because we have to secure all our firearms, and the bunkbeds are important for the boys," Stuart said.

Sandra dished up oatmeal with appropriately sized servings for Stuart and Angel. "I thought I'd make cinnamon toast to go with the oatmeal. Care for any?"

"If our trip goes as well as we expect, we'll be back in time to enjoy cinnamon toast with Henry," Stuart said.

After they ate, Sandra gave Stuart and Angel crackers and dried apples for their backpacks then told them to fill their canteens.

"From now on, whenever someone leaves for a little jaunt, I want them to be ready for an overnight at a minimum," Sandra said.

"What brought this on, Mom?" Stuart asked.

"I had a convoluted dream last night that someone left here after breakfast and didn't come back because they didn't have the resources to be gone overnight; I was convinced it was my fault and spent the rest of the dream trying to make it right. After I woke up in a sweat, I couldn't go back to sleep. I can't let it happen."

"Who was it that left?" Angel asked.

Sandra glowered at them then growled, "You two. You have to promise to come back."

"You know I can't promise that, Mom, but I can promise I'll do everything in my power to keep Angel safe," Stuart said.

"I knew that, but thanks for reminding me because Angel will do the same." Sandra's voice quivered.

"We have to go," Angel said.

"That's my girl," Stuart said as they pulled on their jackets and backpacks then picked up their rifles.

Angel kissed Sandra's cheek, then they left.

"You surprised Mom when you kissed her," Stuart said as they jogged their warmup on the driveway.

"She needed it," Angel said. "Go."

She took off, and Stuart grumbled, "I always fall for that."

He pushed to catch up with her, but she stayed one step ahead of him. When he came close to passing her, she took off.

He grinned. *That's my Angel.*

When they reached Major's house, Angel turned and held up her arms in triumph, and Stuart swept her up and ran with her to the house. Before he set her down on her feet, he spun around with his back to the house, and laughed. "I win."

"You cheated," Angel said.

"Not any more than you do when you say, 'Go' before I'm ready," Stuart said.

Major and Jack came out of the house. "Nice to hear that you two are as competitive as ever," Major said. "What's up?"

Stuart felt his cheeks warm. "We're here to pick up clothes for a little girl we came across yesterday."

"We need to talk to you," Angel said.

Stuart stared at Angel then explained about the two teams that were headed toward them then said, "We think Scooter is the doctor from Atlanta they are supposed to kidnap. We don't think they know exactly where he is, but they must have a pretty good idea because they are headed straight toward us."

"We can defend the farms against the first team, but the second one will hit us less than a day later, and we won't be able to stop them: they will overrun us," Angel said.

"Are they that strong?" Major asked.

"At least from what we've heard on the radio, we suspect they are from the sheer numbers alone," Stuart said. "We're going to meet with Phil and Scooter and the group at our place after we get back, so we can decide what we should do; so far, we've reassessed our defense and have others assessing Leo's farm. Angel wanted to talk to you too."

"We will need to beef up our security..." Major paused and narrowed his eyes. "Are you thinking what I'm thinking, Jack?"

Jack nodded. "What's your plan, Angel?"

"We turn them against each other."

"Be right back." Major strode into the house.

"Where's he going?" Stuart asked.

"He's checking with Mr. Young," Angel said.

When Major returned, he said, "I asked Mr. Young how tight the two teams were, and he told me the second team has orders to bypass the first team then come after Scooter ahead of them, but he doesn't think there is any love lost there. When I told him what Aimee Louise said, he said, 'Yes.'"

Stuart smiled.

"So how do we do that?"

Stuart exhaled. "Stealing trucks has become our specialty. With a little help from our ham operators, we could steal a truck from one of the teams and stir them up against the other team."

"And while we're there, we can steal a truck from the other team in retaliation then leave them to sort it out," Jack said.

"Yes," Angel said.

Jack said 'we;' he's planning to go with us.

"When do we leave?" Jack asked.

"We'll need to finalize our team, plan our assignments, and determine the estimated locations and speeds of our two teams," Stuart said.

"As soon as possible," Angel said. "Are you on the team, Uncle Jack?"

Jack's eyes twinkled. "Yes."

"We'll pick you up after lunch," Angel said.

Stuart glanced at Angel. *She wants to talk to Jack.* "I'll pick up the clothes from Charo then be right back."

CHAPTER FIVE

After Stuart left, Jack asked, "Can you brief me on what you have in mind? Let's sit on the porch."

"I'm interested too." Major joined them.

"We'll need two drivers, two passengers to ride shotgun, and one person to manage our radio communications and to bolster the confusion."

"I'll ask Mr. Young if the two groups have code names or anything for each other," Major said.

"You'd want either Stuart or me to manage the radio communication," Jack said.

"Yes, we need a male voice with authority. Stuart can run almost as fast as I can, so he'll be my passenger. Stuart and I will steal the first truck from the team that we're calling the second one, then take the truck to a meeting point for Andy to drive away with Red as his shotgun passenger. Stuart and I will run back and steal the second truck from the team that is closest to us, then we'll pick you up as we leave. We'll want to do all this at night, so tomorrow night is my target, depending on how far away they are. I don't know if we want to take 48-4 part way to save some travel time and to carry any extra equipment and supplies, but my preference would be to travel by foot and carry what we need."

Jack nodded. "We should travel at least half way then stop for the rest of the night. Tomorrow afternoon we could locate the two teams then wait for nightfall and pick our time to begin based on their routines."

"We know half of the first team has been lining up for a meal before sundown while the other half sets up camp, and they had a lackluster security detail, but that may have changed. We don't have any information about how the second team operates," Angel said.

"More for Mr. Young and Leo to tackle," Major said. "I'll let them know."

"I'll ask Red what the weather will be like for the next three days, but we should prepare for a sudden cold snap and snow," Angel said.

Stuart carried a large duffel bag when he joined them. "Charo had everything packed up for us. Thank goodness it has shoulder straps."

"I'll carry your backpack," Angel said.

"It'll be easier if I hold it up for you, Stuart." Jack picked up the bag. "This is heavy. What on earth is in here?"

"We have a twelve year old boy who found a young girl about four or five years old that was alone in the woods for a while; she was wearing a thin T-shirt and shorts. We know she understands us, but she's not talking at all, so we don't know her name. We don't have any clothes for her, so we asked for anything that Dolly or the twins had outgrown."

"You sure got a haul, didn't you?" Major shook his head.

After Stuart had the shoulder straps in place, he shifted the weight. "Okay, I'm ready, but I can't run, Angel."

"Maybe we should put some of the clothes into a smaller bag that I can carry," Angel said.

"Good idea." Stuart eased the heavy load off his back to the ground. "I felt like I was going to fall over backwards."

"Be right back," Major said.

Major returned with two backpacks. After they had stuffed the larger backpack then put the rest of the items into the other one, Major said, "You'll have to carry your backpacks, but at least you won't have back strain tomorrow."

After they jogged down the driveway to the road, Angel said, "We should walk; the straps on the backpacks aren't very wide and would rub our shoulders raw before we were home."

"You're right. If we're going to carry what we need, we'll have to find my old hiking backpacks," Stuart said.

"We may have to travel lighter than we originally thought."

"It would be ideal if we found a barn where we could sleep a few hours, but it wouldn't be worth the extra time and effort to search for one. I have all kinds of ideas, but none of them are very plausible," Stuart said.

"We'll ask the team." After they arrived at the farmhouse, Stuart said, "You were right about the straps rubbing because I can feel the irritation already, and we took it easy."

When they went inside, Sandra's eyes widened. "Are there any clothes left for the girls at the Cabellos'?"

Stuart chuckled. "You'll probably want to sort these by size. Charo said most of these things were clothes for the twins, but there are a few things that Dolly has outgrown."

"The girls are waiting upstairs, I'll haul these bags upstairs, then we'll pick out clothes for today."

"We'll take them up, Mom," Stuart said. "These backpacks are heavy. We'll carry them to the bedroom door, then you can slide them in."

After they put down the backpacks, Red called out, "I have news from Mr. Young."

Angel and Stuart rushed to their bedroom.

"Mr. Young said that the sheriff confiscated his white truck to go south, and the sheriff claimed he's following the rules," Red said.

Stuart chuckled. "We've shifted from our original plan to travel light to having a full supply of food and ammunition. I'll bet it was Mr. Young's idea in collaboration with Molly. That takes care of my worries about spending the next three days carrying the sleeping gear and extra food we would need."

"What's the weather going to be like between here and the middle of the state over the next three days?" Angel asked.

"We'll get a blast of cold from a northwest wind sometime tomorrow; it will hit us first then roar into middle Georgia, so expect the cold weather to travel with us," Red said. "We'll be coming back in a strong headwind: the kind that takes our breath away. It will be rough."

"Is it smart for you to go?" Angel asked.

Red glared at Angel then exhaled. "It will be particularly difficult for me because my appetite and stamina are down. I've been sneaking in naps when I can. I want to go, but I don't want to drag down the team. If I don't go, someone else has to cover for me, and I hate that. I'd feel like I let Andy down. What would you do?"

"Talk to Mama Sandra."

"You're right." Red left the radio room.

Stuart hugged Angel. "I didn't even consider the challenges that Red would be facing. I held my breath when you asked her if she should go. I wouldn't say she is irreplaceable, but she has a lot of very unique skills that I've been taking for granted."

Angel kissed Stuart then picked up the headset and turned in her swivel chair to face the ham radio.

Stuart watched while Angel took notes and adjusted dials. After a few minutes, she removed her headset. "The cow's in the corn."

Stuart chuckled. "Phil and his family are on the move. They should be at Leo's soon."

Red came into the bedroom. "Mama Sandra listened to me then asked me what everyone always said about me. All I could think of was 'Red has snacks', and she told me I was right. She told me I needed to forget about full meals and snack at least every two hours and my energy level and my sassy confidence will return. We don't have to replace me because I have snacks."

"Take over the radio and have a snack; we just heard that Phil and his family are on their way to Leo's," Angel said.

Before Red picked up the headset, she said, "I realized we have another benefit with the white truck. Mr. Young will make sure it has a mobile radio in good operational order."

"That's huge," Stuart said. "We'll be in contact with the home front."

They stopped for their rifles and jackets before they left the house; Stuart pushed himself to keep Angel in sight while she raced to Leo's. After he reached Leo's driveway, Angel dashed into the house.

Stuart listened as the transport truck rumbled past the driveway on the road. The truck creaked as it crossed the ditch then followed David's circuitous path while the engine hummed as it maneuvered the path along the temporary driveway. Cal climbed out of the passenger's seat then served as a spotter while David backed the truck close to the farmhouse back door.

I didn't even think about who would drive the truck here. Stuart smiled. *Not my job; Angel keeps track of everything, and Red has a list and snacks.*

* * *

Angel came out of the house and joined Stuart. "Leo and I went over the plan for the next few days. He'll follow Mr. Young's lead as far as the radio is concerned. I'll tell you the rest after we unload the truck. Leo asked me to give Deana and Scooter's wife a tour of the house, so they could decide where they wanted things before all their boxes are stacked in the kitchen."

After Deana climbed out of the truck, Scooter's wife handed the baby to her, then Deana joined Angel.

"It's good to see you again, Angel." Deana smiled.

"Hi, Angel. I'm Joyce; it's really nice to meet Dad's Angel, but I feel like I already know you." Joyce lifted her toddler out of the truck, and he clung to her leg.

"Mr. Leo asked me to give you a tour of the house," Angel said.

"Lead on," Deana said.

Joyce took the toddler by the hand, and they followed Angel and Deana.

"I'll show you the second floor first; there are four bedrooms and two bathrooms," Angel said. "There is a master bedroom downstairs."

"There are beds in these bedrooms," Deana said.

"I think the sheets are in the closets; Leo said they are clean," Angel said.

When they reached the third bedroom, Deana said, "This is as large as a master bedroom." After she examined the room, she said, "Joyce, this is a second master bedroom; it has a bathroom attached with a walk-in shower and a big tub."

"We could put both of the children in the bedroom next to us, or next to the master bedroom," Joyce said.

"Leo doesn't use the downstairs master bedroom," Angel said. "He has a pulldown bed in his radio room. I think the upstairs master bedroom was always Jennie's until she became so ill, then Leo moved her downstairs, so he could look after her."

After they went downstairs, Deana inspected the master bedroom and bath, the second downstairs bedroom, and the guest bathroom. "Was this house ever a bed and breakfast?" Deana asked.

"I'm not sure, but it certainly looks like it could be, doesn't it?"

Deana stopped and peeked into the living room. "Love the fireplace."

When they returned to the kitchen, Deana pointed. "There's plenty of room to set up a little kids' play area in that corner. The kitchen is a cook's dream."

Joyce nodded. "I'm in awe of all the counter space for prep work, and the kitchen table is huge. Is there a dining room?"

"I think that may have been the original purpose of Leo's radio room," Angel said.

"First load of boxes coming in," Phil called out.

"Kitchen," Deana said.

After all the boxes were unloaded, Deana said, "That went really smoothly. I'm sorry all those boxes had to go upstairs, but with them out of the major thoroughfare, I can unpack at my leisure."

"I'll park the truck, then Cal and I are heading back. Phil, walk with us to the driveway, and I'll show you the path we use for our shortcut. It goes to the Smith barn then on to the Newtons'; the Smith homestead burned down years ago. Let me know if you want the chicken coop repaired. It won't take much."

"Chicken coop?" Deana asked. "Are there any chickens here?"

"No, but if you're interested after the coop is repaired, you can hatch your own, or someone will give you a few chickens to get you started."

* * *

While Angel gave Deana and Joyce a tour of the house, Stuart and Scooter strolled to the barn.

"The conversation earlier about someone from Atlanta looking for a doctor reminded me of the chief executive officer at the hospital where I worked; he was rumored to have ties to an Atlanta drug cartel, but I always assumed it was gossip. The week before the grid went down, his administrative assistant, who was from Mexico, gave me some papers in a large manila envelope to hold for her; she told me the night cleaning crew found them behind a cabinet in his office, and she was afraid to look at them because she was certain Mr. Ferris would be very angry with her."

Stuart furrowed his brow. "Was he known to have a bad temper?"

"There were stories, but I never paid much attention to them. I locked the envelope in my locker and forgot about it until the grid went down; after a week, everyone had left and not returned except for a few of us in the emergency department, so I took the envelope home and stuck them into an old suitcase. I never bothered to look in the envelope, so for all I know, the papers could be old invoices. I may have thrown out the envelope ages ago, but I don't remember. After we're settled, I'll see if I can find it."

"Angel?" Stuart asked.

"Let's go," she said.

As they ran at Stuart's pace, he said, "It went smoother than I expected. We deserved a break for a change. What did you hear from Leo?"

"Let's stop at the Smith barn and talk," Angel said.

When they reached the barn, Angel said, "The forward group is battalion one, and the other one is battalion two. Andy, as our military history expert, will complain about forty men claiming to be a battalion, but I don't think their leader has military experience. They refer to each other as bats when they are talking within their own group, and Leo said it's meant as a sneer. Does that make sense to you?"

"Yes, they are using bats to mean crazy or incompetent."

Angel shrugged. "I don't get it, but it doesn't matter. Leo said he should have a good idea of their location before we leave. We need to pack for cold weather and have enough food for the five of us for four days, in case we have to hole up somewhere."

"And plenty of snacks for Red," Stuart added.

"Yes, let's go."

Angel set the pace at a speed faster than Stuart's normal pace.

When they reached the farmhouse, Stuart said, "You ran faster than I would have."

"You kept up."

"I did, didn't I? Thanks." Stuart hugged Angel.

"Any time." She giggled. "Was that a good joke?"

Stuart laughed. "It was an excellent joke."

As they went into the house, Mandy and the little girl were drinking milk at the kitchen table. Red came tearing down the stairs, and Andy followed her with a big grin.

"I've been listening for you. We have a big surprise, don't we, girls?"

Mandy and the little girl nodded.

"What's your name?" Red asked as she pointed to Mandy.

"My name is Mandy. What's your name?" Mandy pointed to the little girl.

The little girl giggled. "My name is Red."

Red, Andy, Mandy, and the little girl laughed, then the little girl said, "My name is Aria."

Angel applauded. "What a terrific game. Aria is a beautiful name; it means 'song' in Spanish, doesn't it?"

"Yes." She pointed to Angel. "What's your name?"

"My name is Stuart."

Red, Mandy, Aria, Stuart, and Andy laughed, then Angel said, "My name is Angel."

Sandra came into the kitchen. "You all are playing the name game, aren't you? Red, I'm going to scramble an egg for you and Aria to have as a snack. She needs small, frequent snacks too. I'm pushing protein today. I've been pulling together your snacks for your mission. I'll explain what I've come up with so far after you finish packing your clothes."

"Where are the boys?"

"They went with Farmer Blanche to learn how to milk a cow by starting with a rubber glove. I wouldn't let them make a mess in the kitchen, so they went to the barn after they decided that was the best place to learn how to milk a cow."

"How does that work?" Andy asked.

"Blanche told me they learn to pull down and squeeze. If they just squeeze, they'll make a mess. Mandy, Aria, and I will have our private lesson later. Show Angel your pretty shirt, Aria," Sandra said.

Aria rose from her seat and posed with her hands on her hips then giggled and sat down.

"That is a beautiful pink shirt, and the small red roses remind me of Red," Angel said.

Aria patted the red roses that were embroidered on the neck of her shirt. "This is my pretty shirt."

"Here's your snack, Aria," Sandra said. "Sit down, Red, and you can have your snack too. I made tiny biscuits for you and Aria to go with your tiny snack bite of egg."

After Aria ate her snack, she rose from her seat and took her plate to the sink. "Thank you, Mama Sandra."

"You're very welcome, Aria," Sandra said.

Mandy said, "Let's put on our warm coats, Aria, then we can see how the boys are doing."

Mandy and Aria held hands as they went up the stairs. "We'll do better than the boys, won't we, Mandy?"

Sandra put her hand on her heart. "I love hearing our little chatterbox talk. Mandy started the name game; wasn't that brilliant?"

"Do we know what happened to her parents?" Stuart asked.

Sandra exhaled. "She told Mandy that loud, scary men came to their house, and her mama told her to hide. She ran away as fast as she could then waited for her mama, but she was cold, then Ethan found her."

Louisa came into the kitchen. "Isn't that one of the most heartbreaking stories you've ever heard? That tiny girl is only five years old; can you imagine how her mother must have felt?" Louisa had a catch in her voice. "Mandy told Aria that she made her mama happy because she was so brave."

"Mandy has such a kind heart." Sandra's smile was weak.

"Noel, Mandy, Jimmy, and I had a family meeting, then we invited Aria and Ethan to our meeting and asked them if they would be part of our family. Mandy told Aria that they would be sisters, and Aria hugged Mandy, then when Ethan told Jimmy he'd be his big brother, I thought my heart would burst when they fist-bumped."

"I think that's wonderful," Sandra said.

"Ready to pack?" Andy asked.

"I have our packing list." Red pulled out a folded sheet of paper from her back pocket.

"I was counting on it," Andy said as they headed toward the stairs.

"What would you have done if I didn't have the list yet?" Red asked.

"Waited until you did."

Stuart asked, "Shall we pack, or do we wait for Red's list?"

"We have a copy." Angel handed a sheet of paper to Stuart, then she giggled as she ran for the stairs.

After Stuart and Angel packed, Stuart picked up their backpacks. "We might have to take out a few things because we have to carry everything to Major's house."

"Why would we do that if the sheriff is coming here?" Angel asked.

"That would be ideal, but how do you know the sheriff is coming here?"

When Angel remained quiet, Stuart said, "I missed something, didn't I?"

"Yes."

Mr. Young said something more than what I heard, so tell me what did I miss?"

"Mr. Young said the sheriff confiscated his truck…"

"To go south," Stuart interrupted. "We're south of Major's house, so Jack is coming here. That's what I missed."

Stuart headed toward their bedroom door then stopped and stared at Angel. "I interrupted you. What else did I miss?"

"The sheriff is following the rules. What's our number one rule?"

"No one travels alone," Stuart said automatically. "I get it; if you and I are in one stolen truck, and Red and Andy are in the second one, then Jack would be alone in Mr. Young's old truck. Jack will have someone with him who is most likely an outstanding shot, which means Major, but what about defending Major's and Cabellos' farm?"

Angel shook her head and picked up her heavy, travel backpack then headed downstairs.

Stuart lifted his heavy backpack and exhaled before he followed Angel. *I'm still missing something.*

As he headed toward the kitchen, Stuart paused. *Maybe I'm ignoring the obvious.*

Stuart put his arm around Angel. "I won't like who Jack has with him, will I?"

She kissed him. "No."

"I packed a few things for you to take on your trip." Sandra pointed to the two sturdy wooden crates that were on the kitchen counter.

"Andy might like some help if they packed like we did." Stuart bounded up the stairs then returned with a large, overloaded knapsack. Andy followed Stuart with his backpack, his rifle, and another knapsack that was equally overloaded; Red carried her rifle and her backpack.

"What's in the crates?" Red asked.

"A camping cookstove, cooking pot, frying pan, dishes, plates, and silverware," Sandra said. "I packed bread, crackers, oatmeal, and the soup and chili that Blanche and I canned this summer for meals. I boiled eggs for you, Red, for your snacks with the crackers and packed a carton of eggs for you to scramble or boil for your snacks or meals. Stuart, the box next to the door has gallon jugs of water that your dad filled earlier."

Stuart frowned as he scanned the array of knapsacks, backpacks, and crates. "How were we going to carry all of this gear to Major's farm if Jack wasn't coming here to pick us up?"

Sandra smiled. "Your dad and Cal were ready to load 48-4 and take everything to Major's for you. Are you ready for lunch before the hungry horde sweeps into the kitchen?"

"Lunch sounds good, Mom," Stuart said.

While Stuart and Andy finished their lunch, Scott came into the kitchen.

Angel said, "We need to have lightweight snacks in our backpacks in case we get separated from the sheriff and his truck for a day or overnight."

"I'll pull that together for you, Angel. I'm glad you thought about it," Sandra said.

"So am I, Angel, because Sandra would have thought about it in the middle of the night, and Cal and I would have to find you," Scott said.

After Stuart and Andy finished eating, Scott said, "I have a Georgia map, Angel. Do you think you could give me a general idea of where you think the two battalions are?"

When Scott spread out the map on the table, Red hurried upstairs to see if Leo or Mr. Young had any updates.

Angel pointed at the map as she spoke. "The progress of the first battalion was slow until yesterday. They've sped up quite a bit, and they are here, about forty miles north of the Valdosta interstate exit. I don't think they can keep up the pace today though because they haven't adjusted their overall routine; instead, at least from what we're hearing on the radio, they've cut back and even cut out water and rest breaks rather than start a little earlier and continue to travel a little later in the evening. I don't think they are appropriately physically conditioned or disciplined to do any of that successfully. They still are unloading the entire contents of their two trucks at every overnight stop, which I don't understand at all. We heard there were several deserters yesterday, and that's new. The second battalion, though, is about ninety miles north of Valdosta and is much more disciplined and moves faster than the first one. I think the second battalion will catch up to the first one by Monday or Tuesday. Mr. Young and Leo are tracking both of them very closely with the spotters the ham operators have in place."

Red joined them. "Mr. Young thinks the first battalion plans to continue moving south, so they can travel on a major interstate to go west. Leo said the hams are putting more spotters south of Valdosta on notice to keep track of the bats; Leo is very interested in whether the second battalion follows the first or turns west when they reach Valdosta."

"That definitely makes a difference for us," Stuart said. "Our plan depends on the second group to follow the first."

"We can adjust our plan," Angel said, and Andy nodded.

"You two have already thought about this?" Scott raised his eyebrows.

"Not me, even though I'd like to pretend I did, but if Angel says we can adjust, then I agree," Andy said, and Stuart chuckled.

Sandra pointed to the counter. "I have four stacks here, so each one of you has food for a full day. It's mostly carbs because they are lightweight, except Red has a little extra protein."

While Angel, Red, Stuart, and Andy added the food to their backpacks, Brandon and Henry rush into the house. "Sheriff's here in a big white truck."

"You'll be home for Christmas, won't you, Mama Angel?" Henry asked as she hugged him.

"I'll do everything in my power to get her back to you before Christmas." Stuart hugged Henry and Angel.

"Thanks, Dad," Henry said as Angel kissed his forehead.

"Let's load up," Stuart said.

Mandy, Aria, Louisa, and Blanche came into the house.

"We've got company," Mandy said.

When Stuart opened the door, he narrowed his eyes and whispered, "You were right; this is a terrible idea, and I have no idea what Jack was thinking."

Scott hurried to the door. "Come on in; you're going too, Annie?"

Jack nodded. "She's our best shot and knows the radio as well as Red does."

"How old is Annie?" Stuart whispered.

"Fourteen," Red said.

"How old were you when you harvested your first deer, Stuart?" Blanche asked.

"I was nine, but this is different," Stuart said.

Andy shook his head at Stuart as Red narrowed her eyes then hissed, "Explain how this is different."

Stuart glanced at Annie, Blanche, Red, Louisa, and Angel, who stared at him. *She's studying my cloud.*

He cleared his throat then mumbled, "Shooting a deer is different than shooting a man."

"You're absolutely right, Stuart, but Annie has been on our defense team as a key shooter since she was twelve," Jack said.

"Glad we cleared the air," Scott said. "I'll help you load up."

"Can I talk to you for a minute, Jack?" Sandra asked, and the two of them went into the living room.

"Thanks, Red," Annie said.

"When I first met Dolly, she told me boys were stinky; I think she was right." Red said, and Annie giggled.

Stuart and Andy each picked up a crate. As they carried them outside, Andy whispered, "I was afraid Red was going to shoot you for a minute there."

"So was I," Stuart whispered. "We need a signal you can give me to shut my trap."

"I seriously considered yelling, 'Man down,' but that might have been too noticeable."

Stuart snorted. "It probably would have gone over my head."

Andy chuckled as Jack joined them.

CHAPTER SIX

"Do you have extra food in all of your backpacks in case we are separated?" Jack asked.

"Sure do," Stuart said. "Who won the bet?"

"Major," Jack grumbled. "I thought Molly was the only person in the world who was that overprotective. Josh wanted to know if you have one or two camping stoves."

"We have two," Stuart said.

"Mr. Young will be sad to hear that." Jack chuckled.

"What does the winner get with your bets?" Andy asked.

"Josh and Mr. Young bet chores; Major and I bet bragging rights. We used to bet desserts, but Molly caught on," Jack said.

"Both of you lost your dessert rights for a week?" Stuart asked.

"To quote Angel, 'Yes.'"

"Do we expect rain, Red?" Jack asked as Red and Angel carried out their backpacks.

"No, but snow for Christmas is a strong possibility. Our weather will turn cold on Monday or Tuesday."

"Mr. Young told me about the latest potential split of the two bats, Stuart. Do we head east or south?" Jack asked.

Stuart glanced at Angel.

"East on the backroads," she said.

"What's our seating arrangement?" Jack asked.

"Stuart and I will sit in the front with you; Stuart will take the window, and I'll be on the radio. In the back seat, Annie and Andy will sit at the windows, and Red in the middle, so she can take notes. Annie and Red can switch off to give Red a break. We'll need meticulous notes, so we can track the two groups as closely as possible. We'll want to know the second they deviate from their expected path," Angel said.

"I'm glad you'll be in the front seat, Angel, because you see things the rest of us miss," Jack said.

"Annie has a good eye too," Angel said. "Be sure to listen to what she says."

Stuart sighed. "Let me know if you have any hints on listening; right now, my best skill is jumping to wrong conclusions."

Scott and Blanche carried plastic bins when they came out of the house.

Scott set his long plastic bin on the tailgate of the truck. "Noel wanted to know if you're set with ammo, and it kind of doesn't matter what you say because Noel packed ammo and a couple of extra rifles and pistols for you."

"These are old quilts." Blanche set her large bin next to the bin packed by Noel. "Sandra and I decided the ground might be cold, so we gathered up quilts for extra padding under your sleeping bags."

"We should probably leave before Doc Larkin decides he's going along as our medical team," Andy said.

"Please assume your assigned seats, and let's hit the road," Jack said.

"How do we keep all the extra gear dry if it rains?" Stuart asked as they headed east.

"Major and Josh put in large tarps. We even have an extra fifteen gallons of diesel for this old truck." Jack pointed to the dash. "Mr. Young sent you a set of earbuds, so you could listen to the radio with the headset, earbuds, or over the speaker, Angel."

In the middle of the afternoon, Jack slowed then pulled into a driveway that was overgrown with grass and weeds. "We need a stretch break, and I got an in depth lecture from Sandra about Red's snacks."

"Sorry," Red said. "I should have warned you."

"Molly was the same, Red, so don't worry about it; I'm glad Sandra was there to help you."

While Red ate her snack, everyone else stretched and drank water.

"I'd like to find them before dark, so we can see if they've made any changes to their routine," Angel said.

"How close do you want the truck?" Jack asked after they were back on the road.

"Close enough that Red and I can run to observe them after they've stopped, but not in the direct path of their morning route."

Jack nodded. "Do we know yet what their morning route will be?"

"Not yet," Angel said.

"If we're northwest of them when we stop for the night, we won't be in their way whether then go west or south," Stuart added.

Red leaned forward. "After Angel and I pinpoint them this evening, we may have a good idea of where they plan to stop tomorrow night."

"What about the second battalion?" Andy asked.

Jack exhaled. "They're still our wild card. We'll wait to hear from Mr. Young and Leo."

After Annie and Andy lowered their windows a few inches, Stuart heard them whispering, so he glanced back at them.

Andy's face was drawn. "Jack, is there a town ahead of us?"

"About six miles ahead, why?"

"We need to divert around it. Annie and I have noticed several deer in the ditches alongside the road the last few miles. Locals wouldn't leave a dead deer alongside the road; they would have taken it home and prepared it for food. We don't know who killed the deer or when, but it was probably fairly recent because we didn't smell any dead animals; Annie and I think it's very possible there's a gang that's either holed up in town or has an ambush set up right outside of town for any travelers."

Jack pulled over as Angel and Stuart examined the map.

"We found a possible detour, but it takes us closer to the interstate than we planned," Stuart said as Angel pointed to the map then handed it to Jack.

"They have stayed on the interstate so far," Jack said. "What do you think?" Jack handed the map to Red.

"What do you two think?" Red asked the backseat companions.

"Dad's right; this first group has stayed close to the interstate; our only potential problem would be deserters, but I think they'd be more likely to head north for Atlanta or the mountains or east for the coast rather than south or west, which is the direction the group is headed," Annie said.

"I agree, Annie," Andy said. "Looks like we'll be a little less than five miles from the interstate. Would we want to stop and let them come to us?"

"That might be a good idea," Jack said. "We can save our fuel and energy and let them burn theirs."

"I'll check with Mr. Young to see if there are any updates on their speed or location," Angel said.

"Our detour is about a mile ahead," Stuart said as Jack pulled back onto the road.

"Here it is." Stuart pointed at the upcoming dirt road on their right.

After Jack turned onto the rough road, Stuart glanced at Andy, who had put his arm around Red to keep her from being too jostled by the rough road.

Jack slowed as he avoided the worst of the ruts. After several miles, the dirt road intersected with another dirt road then became a narrow, paved road with a few potholes.

"Snack time," Annie announced. "Here you go, Red."

"Mama Sandra put you in charge of my snacks?" Red asked.

Annie giggled. "Sure did."

"I'll bet you volunteered," Red growled.

"Thank you, Annie," Andy said. "I appreciate you."

"You would," Red mumbled as she nibbled on her crackers and goat cheese. "Is this your goat cheese?"

"Yep, Mom and I made it this past week. What do you think?"

"It's really good, but pretend I didn't say that because I want to be cranky."

Jack snorted. "You're doing great so far, Red."

"There's a man standing in the middle of the road in front of us. He has a cane and is cradling his rifle," Angel said. "He's not dangerous."

"I'll slow down, but everyone be prepared for me to slam down on the accelerator if there's an ambush."

"Shooters, be ready, but keep your rifles low and out of sight," Stuart said.

As Jack slowed and moved to the middle of the road, the man stepped back to the shoulder on the driver's side of the truck. Everyone lowered their windows.

"He's worried and scared," Angel said.

When Jack reached the man, he stopped.

"Thank you, mister," the man said. "I took a chance that y'all weren't with the thugs who have been terrorizing the farms around here. My house was back in these here woods, but a mob broke in two days ago. My wife and I were working the garden and made it to our root cellar behind our barn before they knew we were there. We was sure glad our old dog followed Mama. They burned down our house and took our cow. Our chickens ran away from them but came back to roost last night, and mama caught them all and put them in our old dog's kennel. I need to get word to my son to come get us."

"Where's your son?" Jack asked.

"He's only ten miles away, but I can't walk that far, and I told Mama she couldn't go off on her own, but she loaded the kennel of chickens onto her garden wagon and is ready to leave with the dog." The man sighed. "She told me I'm out of touch with modern women, and she's not listening to any more of my foolishness."

Jack handed the map to the man. "Can you show me where your son lives on the map?"

The man pointed. "Right about here."

Angel peered at the map then leaned close to Stuart and whispered, "On our way."

"Andy and I could ride in the back," Stuart whispered.

Angel shook her head. "You, Annie and I ride in the back with the chickens; Red can ride in the front with Jack, and Andy can ride in the back with the older couple and their dog."

Stuart frowned. *She has a good reason. She'll tell me later.*

* * *

After Stuart and Andy left to go with the man to help his wife with the chickens, Angel told Jack, Red, and Annie the travel plans.

"You see the two men hiding in the tall grass ahead?" Annie asked.

"Yes."

"Why haven't they ambushed us?" Jack asked. "I would have thought they would have ambushed us as soon as we stopped or when Stuart and Andy left."

"I don't know, but the old man knows. I'm sure he or his wife will tell Stuart and Andy before they return."

Annie faced Jack. "Five men."

"I won't stare," Jack said. "Are they on both sides of the road?"

Annie nodded. "They're moving closer to the road."

"Can I stand in the back of the truck and pick them off before Andy and Stuart get back?" Red asked.

"Tempting," Jack said, "but no."

"What if Annie helps me?"

"Still a no," Jack said.

While they were waiting, Stuart strolled down the driveway; Angel raced to him, and he hugged her.

"The old man told us that the gang of men thinks the old woman has a still, which has been a local joke for years because her grandfather was the most famous bootlegger in three counties during prohibition, and her father ran the still for years after he came back from World War II, according to her husband."

"Is there a still?" Angel asked.

"No, the woman sold it to a collector years ago to fund their three children's college educations."

Stuart kissed Angel then strolled toward the driveway while Annie joined Angel.

"There might be a dozen men. Red's still arguing with Dad, and he's loving it. Mom always says Dad is a terrible tease." Annie giggled. "It's kind of fun watching him in action."

"The ambush men are after the old woman because they think she has a still. They are waiting for her."

"That's interesting," Annie said. "I'll let Dad know."

Annie returned to the truck then carried a snack and a cup of water to Red. Jack continued to scan the road ahead with his back to Red and Annie; when he slightly adjusted the bill of his ball cap, Angel smiled. *Annie told him.*

When Red's cranky cloud brightened, Angel shook her head. *Jack and Red came up with a plan, and Red's happy.*

* * *

Stuart and the old woman stirred up the dust on the driveway as they walked toward the truck; the old woman held onto Stuart's arm with her right hand and had her rifle slung over her right shoulder. Stuart carried a tote bag in his left hand and his rifle in his right one. An old, brown dog followed them.

After Stuart helped the old woman into the backseat of the truck, and she slid to the middle of the bench seat, the old brown dog tried to hop into the truck, so Stuart gave him a little assist. Jack stood at his driver's door, and Red climbed into the passenger's seat while Annie and Angel climbed into the back of the truck with their rifles. Angel stood next to the cab, midway between the two sides, and Annie knelt on the driver's side of the truck bed midway between the cab and the tailgate.

Stuart stopped at the back of the truck. "Do we have a plan?"

"Sure do. I'll tell both of you when we're all in the back," Annie said.

Stuart sauntered to the driveway and took over pulling the wagon from Andy. Andy helped the old man into the truck on the passenger's side then went around the truck and climbed into the backseat behind the driver. Stuart handed the kennel with the complaining chickens to Angel, who set the chickens on top of one of the crates then began rearranging the boxes around her.

"Hang on, girls," Annie said. "We're in for a ride."

Stuart rolled his eyes and chucked the wagon into the truck, upside down on a knapsack.

After he jumped into the truck, Annie said, "Dad's going to start off slow then stomp the accelerator to throw them off, so be ready for it. Red's telling Andy to shoot anyone who aims a gun. Dad said to knock on the top of the cab twice when we're ready."

"We'll follow Red's advice," Stuart said. "Are you okay with that, Annie?"

"Oh, yes."

Stuart knelt down. "We're ready, Angel."

Angel pounded twice on the top of the cab then braced herself between her boxes as Jack began his slow pace.

"The slow-moving truck is drawing them out of the high grass." Angel peered over the top of the cab. "Annie's estimate of a dozen men is correct. Expect acceleration in three, two, one, now."

When the truck jerked forward, everyone was braced and ready. The men who were standing in the middle of the road stared at the speeding truck at it came straight at them then yelled before they scrambled to the ditch. Men who were still in the field shouted and aimed at the truck as it sped toward them even faster, and Stuart, Red and Andy fired, then Annie fired.

Angel turned toward the rear and fired at the men who ran out behind them with raised rifles.

Stuart cringed at the sound of several plunks on the truck's body, but as the truck roared away, Stuart saw men on the ground and watched the others as they ran away from the truck and the road.

"Anybody hit?" Stuart called out.

"I'm not," Annie said.

"We're all okay up here," Red shouted.

Stuart's eyes widened and his heart raced when he scanned where Angel had been standing. He shouted, "Angel, I don't see you. Are you okay?"

"Daddy, stop! Angel's down!" Annie screamed.

Jack pulled over and jumped out of the driver's seat while Stuart scrambled to the boxes that had shifted on top of where Angel had been standing. Red struggled to undo her seatbelt then leapt out of the passenger's seat and tripped, but Andy had raced around the front of the truck and caught her. He held onto her as they hurried to the back of the truck. Andy lifted Red into the back of the truck then jumped in and held onto her, so she wouldn't get in Stuart's way while he frantically searched for Angel.

Tears blinded Stuart as he pulled away boxes; he exhaled when he saw Angel huddled in a small open space.

"The boxes knocked me down." She pointed at the box above her head. "Look at that."

The bullet hole in the box three inches above Angel's head took away Stuart's breath, and he sank to his knees next to her then grabbed onto her.

"I love the boxes that knocked you down." Tears continued to stream down his face.

"Is Angel okay?" Jack asked as he scrambled across the boxes to them.

"I'm fine," Angel said.

"Look at this." Stuart wiped away the tears with his shirtsleeve.

Jack inspected the bullet hole then gazed at Stuart. "Are you going to be okay? Do we turn back?"

"We don't turn back," Angel growled.

Stuart stared at her then swallowed hard. "Okay, we keep going, but if I have one more scare like this, we're going back."

"I agree; no arguments, no discussion: we go back," Jack said.

Stuart helped Angel up, then Andy coaxed Red and Angel out of the back of the truck, so he and Stuart could rearrange the boxes and calm the frightened chickens.

* * *

Annie brought her backpack and rifle along with her as she climbed out of the truck and joined Angel and Red.

"Let's sit under the tree," Red said. "My knees are weak."

"Snack for all three of us." Annie handed Red a boiled egg then gave Red and Angel crackers with goat cheese and kept two for herself.

"That stuff about no arguments and no discussion was an overreaction," Red said. "They'll get over it, but don't do it again because it was too scary."

Annie watched Andy as he returned to the back of the truck to talk to the older couple.

"Andy is talking to the older people and their dog to calm them down. It must have been scary for them too because all of us were screaming, except Angel," Annie said.

"Actually, I tried to answer Stuart when he asked if I was okay, but the boxes had knocked the breath out of me, and all I could do was squeak," Angel said.

"Let's load up," Red announced in her command voice, and Annie giggled as she held out her hand to help up Red from the ground.

"Same positions?" Annie asked as they headed to the truck.

"Same positions," Angel said.

"Except for the being buried alive in boxes part," Red added as she elbowed Angel, and Annie giggled.

* * *

Stuart watched as Angel, Red, and Annie hurried to the truck. *Those three are so resilient. They've bounced right back, and I'm still a basket case.*

Jack put his hand on Stuart's shoulder. "Are you doing okay?" he asked quietly.

"Not at all." Stuart exhaled. "That was all my nightmares come to life in a split-second."

Jack nodded. "You give the word, and I'll turn the truck around; no questions asked."

Stuart chuckled. "I wouldn't put you through that torture. I have a feeling you'd have three to take on."

"Annie has always looked up to Angel and Red, so she's in heaven because they are treating her like a peer," Jack said.

"That's how Angel and Red are, isn't it? They've always been really close, but they have plenty of room to pull in others."

"Let's hit the road and get these good people to their son's house." Jack strode to the driver's seat and turned on the engine; everyone scrambled to their assigned positions.

When they reached the driveway that the old man said went to his son's house, Jack pulled into the driveway then stopped and lowered his window as Stuart hopped out of the truck and joined Jack at the driver's side.

"How far away is the house?" Stuart asked.

"It's just around the curve," the man said.

"Could you make it on your own from here if we load the chickens into your wagon for you? We'd like to be on our way if you'll be okay," Jack said.

"That sounds great. Our son would have all kinds of questions, and his wife would want you to stay for a bite to eat, which is a full feast at her house. She's a fabulous cook, but not quite as good as Mama."

"I'll get the wagon and the chickens. They're going to walk to the house from here," Stuart said.

"We need to go with them," Angel said.

Just this once, I'm going with what Angel said and not try to put my own spin on it.

"Who goes?" Stuart asked as Jack joined them.

"I had an elaborate plan in my head, but it would be better if you could stall the parents here while Red and I get a quick look at the house," Angel said.

When Red heard her name, she climbed out of the truck with her rifle. "Ready when you are."

* * *

Angel and Red silently raced into the woods. Angel motioned to the left, and Red peeled away from her to circle the house. When Angel was close to the house, she slowed her pace then crept closely enough to have a clear view of the front yard.

Six men with danger clouds. The young man on the ground has been badly beaten, but he's feigning unconsciousness.

Angel mimicked the lonely-sounding call of a barred owl then heard a cardinal song behind her.

She smiled. *Stuart's signature call.*

She backed away from the house and joined Stuart. "Six men; danger clouds," she whispered. "Battered young man on the ground; he's pretending to be unconscious."

"Red found a young woman with a baby hiding in the woods near the road; she'll take them to the truck then bring Andy here. Do you think we can take them?"

Angel nodded. "I saw an old oak on this side of the driveway that would give Andy a clear view of the house if he climbs it; he'd be hidden in the foliage. Red can be on the same side as Andy but low behind some snags. After you see where they are, position yourself on the other side of the driveway to make sure no one gets a clear shot at either of them. I'll start a diversion behind the house out of everyone's range of fire. Don't let any of the danger men leave the front yard."

"I have to be where you are," Stuart said. "Are we at the front or back?"

Angel exhaled. "We can't create a diversion and cover Andy and Red simultaneously. We'll have to take down all of the danger men at the same time."

"Then that's what we'll do," Stuart growled.

Angel stared at his cloud. *His protective cloud is practically on fire.*

"Yes."

Stuart disappeared then reappeared. "Andy and Red are getting into place. I told them to wait until they hear our diversion. Where will we be?"

"At the entrance from the driveway to the front yard behind the decorative brick wall."

"I'll let them know. Don't move without me."

When Stuart returned, Angel said, "Run to the driveway and make lots of noise."

While she and Stuart crashed through the bushes toward the driveway entrance, the men shouted, and Andy and Red fired as Angel and Stuart reached the brick wall; Stuart fired at a man who was aiming high in the tree where Andy was perched, and the man dropped to the ground.

Angel watched as one of the men who had fallen near the porch when the gunfire first started began shifting his weight then slowly inched toward the front door and a rifle. When he almost imperceptibly moved his forefinger to the trigger of a rifle, Angel fired, and his hand fell away from the rifle.

"I didn't notice him," Stuart said. "Cover me."

Stuart slowly walked into the open where Red and Andy could see him.

"Cover him," Angel shouted as she assumed a shooting position then carefully scanned each motionless man that lay on the ground. Stuart knelt next to the young man and whispered then dragged the man to the driveway and behind the brick wall.

"I'm going to check the house." Stuart cautiously avoided the men on the ground as he headed toward the back of the house then came out the front door. "The house is clear. Andy, would you check for any survivors?"

"Will do; Red wants to let Jack and the family know our status; could Angel cover me?" Andy asked.

"I'm ready," Angel said.

When Stuart reached the low brick wall, Angel was moving into position to cover Andy as he began his survey of the downed men, and the young man was leaning against the wall in a sitting position and breathing in shallow, ragged breaths.

CHAPTER SEVEN

"How badly injured are you?" Stuart asked.

"Not nearly as badly as I could have been." The young man tried to suppress his coughs. "After I was sure that Willa and the baby had gotten away safely, I realized these thugs planned to beat me until they got the information they wanted or I was dead, so I played dead."

The man took a few more breaths. "Are you with the militia?"

"No."

"The thugs that attacked me were terrified that the militia was after them, but they aren't; I've been in contact with the militia for quite a while, and there are no units close to here yet. The thugs talked about joining a jitters gang if they could find one before the militia found them. The one who seemed to be the leader said if they had a still they could give Old Jitters, they'd get on his good side. Does any of that mean anything to you?"

Stuart gazed at him. "Were you a cop in your previous life?"

The man started to chuckle but coughed instead and pressed his arm against his chest. "Maybe, but you were too, weren't you? I'm Gabe."

"Stuart." He smiled. "We think Old Jitters is the head of a cartel and is after one of our neighbors; from what we know, Old Jitters sent two battalions of men to kidnap our neighbor and wipe out everyone associated with him; we're not strong enough to fight off the two factions, so we're hoping to turn them against each other."

"That's absolutely brilliant. Your idea?"

Stuart snorted. "Angel's idea; my only brilliant idea was marrying her."

"How can I help?"

"Do you have a ham radio?"

"I'm on several hours a day. I've been hearing a lot of chatter about men with jitters going to southwest Georgia lately, but I never understood whether the men had a nervous condition or were afraid of something specific, but now the pieces are starting to fall into place. So, how can I help?"

"Hams have been tracking the locations and speed of the two factions, but we haven't heard much lately because all we have is a mobile. Are you up to getting on your radio? Angel knows exactly what to listen for, if you don't mind letting her sit with you."

Gabe tried to rise and groaned. "I might need a little help. I don't think they managed to break anything or damage any of my internal organs because I rolled with the punches, but my ribs must be badly bruised."

Stuart provided support for Gabe as he pushed himself to his feet. Gabe gasped when he rose then splinted his ribs with his arms. "Taking a deep breath isn't my best skill right now. Is her name really Angel, or is that your nickname for her?"

Stuart chuckled. "She saved an old ham a few years ago, and he called her his 'Angel'; everyone else picked it up because it fits. Our son calls her Mama Angel."

"Help me get to my radio, and Angel and I will find some answers."

As Stuart and Gabe made their way to the house, Andy asked, "Do you have a large tractor or a backhoe? We don't have any survivors."

"I sure do, but I don't think I could operate it."

"I can," Andy said. "Where is it?"

"In the barn," Gabe said. "My neighbor to the north left two years ago, and his place was burned down not long after he was gone. Anywhere on the property is fine except for near the well."

Andy nodded. "I'll find a spot."

"I'll go with you," Angel said.

"I'll go with him, Angel. You can stay with Gabe while he checks his radio," Stuart said.

"Radio?" Angel bounced on her toes.

"Best that money could buy ten years ago and the same for the antenna." Gabe's smile was weak.

Stuart helped Gabe into the house while Angel quizzed him about his radio.

Stuart rolled his eyes. *I don't understand half of what she's saying.*

When Stuart returned to the front yard, Andy came around the house from the side yard.

"I thought it would be less gruesome for the family if we dragged all the bodies around to the brush before we leave."

"Why don't you check the backhoe, and I'll finish clearing the yard, then we can go," Stuart said.

Andy nodded then trotted off to the barn.

After Stuart dragged the last of the bodies into the brush, he heard the roar of a large tractor. Andy joined him then put the tractor on idle. "We can't tell David about this because he'll bring Brandon and Tracker and move in with these fine folks."

Stuart chuckled. "He might have to wrestle the keys away from Farmer Blanche."

"I don't think we can load all of the deceased into the bucket, even as large as it is, so we'll be making five or six trips."

Andy drove the lumbering tractor to the neighbor's property while Stuart followed.

After they found a cleared area, Andy used the backhoe and dug the deep hole, then the two of them returned. They lifted a body into the bucket, then Stuart followed Andy as he drove to the hole and slid the body into the hole with Stuart's guidance. After all six bodies were in the grave, Andy covered them with dirt then pushed two downed trees over the dirt before he and Stuart headed back.

When they reached the house, Jack and Annie were waiting next to Jack's truck.

"Red joined Angel to take notes. I listened to the radio too while Dad talked to Mr. Gabe and his dad, then Red wanted to talk to Ms. Willa about her baby, so I went with her and listened. Ms. Willa's three brothers are coming here in the morning. One of them is married and will bring his family. They don't live very far away, but Ms. Willa said Mr. Gabe thinks everyone will be safer if they are together and has been after them for a long time to move here. I told Ms. Willa that Thursday is Christmas, and she was very excited because her family will be together for Christmas for the first time in years."

Angel came out of the house. "We need to leave." She climbed into the truck bed, and Annie hopped in too.

"We'll argue later." Red climbed into the front seat of the truck, and Andy slid in next to her.

Jack hurried to the truck, and Angel said, "North about ten miles, then we'll need to find a good spot for the truck to be our base."

Stuart climbed in across from Annie, then Jack drove slowly on the driveway to the road. After Jack accelerated as he headed north, Stuart motioned for Annie to sit on the truck bed then moved closer to Angel; they sat closely huddled, so Angel could speak without shouting over the wind noise.

"The first bat is about thirty miles north of here. The spotters think the leader is not used to making decisions because he has been trying to contact Old Jitters on the common simplex band; they don't expect the first bat to go any more than five more miles before they stop for the day, which is early even for them. The second bat will be within forty miles of them an hour or two after sunset at their current rate of travel, so it depends on when the bat two leader decides to stop."

"Old Jitters must not be close enough to receive a simplex transmission; bat one's leader obviously doesn't have any radio experience," Stuart said.

"The hams certainly thought so too. I told Gabe our plan, and he wants to make sure both battalions are stopped. Gabe and I don't think tonight will be a good night to start stirring things up, after all.

We let Mr. Young know tomorrow night is more likely, but Gabe will continue to listen for us to mention our code word, 'roast beef,' then he'll let Mr. Young and Leo know we're ready for them to build the tension," Angel said.

"How did you come up with such an unusual code word?" Stuart asked.

"I didn't; Mr. Young did," she said.

Stuart returned to his position across from Annie; he scanned the countryside on both sides of the truck as Jack sped to their next destination.

Angel knows how he came up with the code word and opted not to tell me. Wonder who helped him and if I'm mad at Mr. Young.

When Jack slowed then turned, Stuart said, "I'll go with you to watch bat one; I may not be able to run as fast as you and Red, but I can run as far as you can."

"You'll have to hang back while I go close to their camp because you aren't as stealthy as I am."

Stuart exhaled. "You'll have to teach me. Can you teach me before we go?"

"I can show you, but you'll have to practice."

"Me too?" Annie asked.

"Yes."

Stuart exhaled. *Those two just upped the ante on me.*

Jack parked behind an overgrown roadside picnic area that was hidden from the road.

When everyone climbed out of the truck, Stuart said, "This was a fortunate find."

"I take full credit for asking Mama for a recommendation." Jack grinned.

"Dad, Angel's going to teach Stuart and me to be stealthy," Annie said.

"Pressure's on you, Stuart," Red said.

"No kidding," Stuart said, and Andy chuckled.

"We'll stretch and take a water break," Angel said.

"My turn to announce the snack break," Red said. "Did we finish off the goat cheese?"

"Not quite," Annie said. "Mama Sandra made strawberry jam scones for a snack, so we can have scones and goat cheese."

"That sounds good," Red said.

While they munched on their snack and drank water, Andy said, "Your appetite has improved, honey; Mama Sandra was right about the small meals."

"After you train your students, Angel, can Andy and I be the impartial judges on stealth?" Red asked.

"Actually, I want to be a judge too," Jack said.

"Are we ready for that level of scrutiny?" Stuart asked.

"Yes." Annie grinned.

Angel spoke quietly to Jack, and Stuart frowned when Jack smiled then handed Angel a box of ammunition.

"I have some loose ammo for both of you to put into your pockets." Angel handed four bullets to Stuart then to Annie.

"Walk quietly toward the woods and listen."

After they were halfway to the woods, Angel said, "Stop. What did you hear?"

"Birds and the rattling ammo," Annie said.

"Right; the ammo were telling you that you were walking too fast."

Angel bent her knees slightly. "Bend your knees to lower your center of gravity, and you'll be more stable. Place your foot down on the outer edge first then roll the rest of your foot down and put weight on your foot unless you hear a sound then lift your foot and reposition it and try again; take your next step the same way."

"Follow me." Angel slowly walked toward the woods the same way she had showed them. She continued to face the woods when she stopped. "I don't have to turn to know you are right behind me because I heard you. If I have to look back to see if you are there, you pass."

After ten more minutes of practice, Stuart wiped off the sweat from his forehead with his shirtsleeve. "What do you think, Annie? Do we need more time to work on this?"

"Yeah, like a month or two."

Stuart nodded. "We'll practice together. Let's give our ammo back to your dad."

"I'll take it from you," Jack said. "I'll bet both of you are afraid to move right about now."

"Are we that transparent?" Stuart asked, and Annie giggled.

"Is the torture entertainment over?" Red yawned. "I'm claiming the back seat of the truck for a nap."

"I'll be on the radio with Gabe; will that bother you?" Angel asked.

"Not at all," Red said.

"When can we expect the cold weather to hit us?" Jack asked.

"The front won't move in until late tomorrow or early Tuesday." Red climbed into the truck.

"Molly packed canned chicken soup and canned chili for hot meals with biscuits and cornbread to go with them, but I'd like to save them for cold nights. What do we have that would work for tonight?" Jack asked.

"Mama Sandra and Blanche told me we had tamales, precooked taco meat, and small flour tortillas, and we should heat them up in a skillet tonight," Andy said.

"I'll set up the camp stove on the picnic table and be tonight's chef," Jack said.

"Do you feel like a walk to the road, Annie?" Stuart asked. "We'll be a little noisy because we won't walk as quietly as Angel, but we can practice our foot rolls or whatever it's called."

"I'd like that."

After they grabbed their backpacks and jackets, the two of them walked with great care as they put down their feet on the edge then rolled onto the soles of their boots and shifted their weight. They stopped every few feet and listened.

Before they reached the road, Stuart pointed to the grass on the left side of the overgrown path that was once a lane, and Annie made her way into the grass and weeds and crouched down while Stuart assumed the same position on the opposite side of the path.

Stuart listened. *That occasional sound I hear in the distance is traffic on the interstate. I think we're closer than five miles.*

Stuart whistled his cardinal call then slowly rose and sidestepped to the path while he scanned the road and listened; Annie copied him.

They tried a few steps backward with their new way of walking, but it was too difficult to walk and stay aware of their surroundings, so they walked backward as quietly as they could.

"Down," Annie hissed, and Stuart automatically moved to the brush and crouched down as a truck came into view. *A driver, passenger, and two men in the truck bed.*

"What do you think? Is there a house down there?" a man asked.

"Naw; it's too overgrown. Nobody has been there in years."

The truck continued their slow progress down the road.

After Stuart couldn't hear the engine, he waited a few more minutes before he whispered, "Okay."

They went to the picnic table shelter.

"How did your practice go?" Jack asked as he unpacked what he would need to heat up their supper.

"We saw a truck go past the entrance to the picnic area. There were two men in the truck bed." Annie told him what the men said. "I'm going to tell Angel in case she wants to warn Mr. Gabe."

After Annie left, Jack asked, "Did I make a mistake bringing Annie, Stuart? I didn't expect it to be so dangerous."

"I understand what you're saying, but a wise sheriff once told me that there was no future in second-guessing myself. Look at how valuable Annie is to the group. She's an outstanding marksman, and she's had the gumption to take on Red."

"You hit a nerve with that quote; never thought it would come back to haunt me." Jack chuckled. "Annie's meeting Red head-on, isn't she?"

After Red woke from what she called her power nap, Jack warmed their supper while Annie pulled out water for everyone to refill their canteens.

"This is a high-class buffet," Jack said. "Fix your own taco and serve yourself a tamale."

Everyone pulled out their mess kits and served themselves then sat on the large tarp that Andy had put on the ground for their seating area.

"Any updates from Gabe?" Andy asked while they ate.

"Bat one has already unloaded both their trucks for the night, but it took longer than it has lately because of the desertions. Gabe said the spotters estimated only ten percent left, but they must have been doing most of the loading and unloading, so there are fewer hands to do the manual work. The ones that are left seem particularly vicious, and some of the hams wonder if that's the real reason the others left," Angel said.

"What about bat two?" Red asked.

"Bat two's leadership is more experienced, and it shows, according to the hams, but what is important from our point of view is that bat two is still on the move. I'll check in with Gabe before we go to bed, so we'll know where bat two stopped for the night; we may have to adjust our position early tomorrow morning. The spotters think the overall leader is behind bat two somewhere, but no one has seen any signs to back it up."

"Gabe's been a great addition to our communications line," Jack said.

"Willa told me Gabe has been discouraged since the grid went down because he felt like he was powerless, and she's very encouraged by how energized he is with feeling like he's part of a team that is taking down bad guys," Red said.

Stuart nodded. "He was a Georgia state trooper; I understand how he feels."

"What are our sleeping arrangements?" Andy asked.

"After we clear a sleeping area, we can put down our tarp. Mom and Blanche packed a large bin of quilts, so all of us can fold a quilt under our sleeping bags for a little more cushioning," Stuart said.

"We'll take turns standing watch," Jack said. "I want Annie to sleep in the truck."

"No discussion about that, Dad?" Annie asked.

"It's okay, Annie. He's allowed to pull out his dad card once in a while," Red said. "Angel and I have persnickety husbands, so it's only fair that you have a persnickety dad."

"Thank you, Red." Jack rolled his eyes.

Annie giggled, and Stuart elbowed Andy.

"There are five of us, so we could easily cover the watch in one and a half to two-hour shifts, but how do we tell the time?" Andy asked.

"We set up the order of the shifts," Angel said.

"What if some certain person won't relinquish the shift to the next person and stays up all night?" Red asked.

Jack smiled. "When the person who follows your certain person wakes up, she can tell him to go to sleep."

"Other way too, right?" Andy asked.

"Yes," Angel said.

"Our most logical order is Stuart, Angel, Andy, Red, then me," Jack said.

"You're going to follow me?" Red asked. "That's not fair; you'll cut my shift short."

Andy smiled. "I like it."

"Where's the best area to clear?" Angel asked.

Stuart snorted. *Leave it to Angel to step into the middle of an argument and cut it short.*

Stuart and Andy found a small clearing on the edge of the woods. After everyone pitched in to clear the area of sticks and rocks, they put the largest tarp into place then placed their sleeping bags on quilts.

"Mama Sandra packed dessert for us," Red said. "I need hot tea with mine."

"What's for dessert?" Andy asked as he placed a pan of water on a camp stove burner to heat.

Stuart used the other camp stove and their small tin coffee pot to make coffee for Jack and himself.

"I don't know; Blanche told me they are labeled, so we're having our Sunday dessert," Red said.

Angel pulled out a covered pan labeled 'Sunday' then handed it to Annie who peeked to see what their Sunday dessert was.

"We have peach cobbler." Annie set the pan on the picnic table.

After the coffee perked and the tea steeped, everyone helped themselves to cobbler.

While they ate, Andy said, "Sometime we need to go on a camping trip that doesn't involve bad guys."

"We'd be bored," Red said.

* * *

While it was still dark, Stuart woke to the bubbly sound of percolating water as it heated in the old tin coffee pot. He slipped out of his sleeping bag and joined Jack at the table.

"Did you shorten Red's shift?" Stuart quietly asked as Jack poured their coffee.

"As much as I dared."

While they sipped their coffee in comfortable silence, Angel joined them. "I'd like to listen to the radio while I wait for Gabe. Should I wait until later, so I don't wake Annie?"

"She'll be fine; she may stay in the truck with you and listen," Jack said.

After Angel left for the truck, Jack said, "Molly packed quite a few eggs for us. I think I'll scramble up eggs; we may not have the luxury of a warm breakfast tomorrow."

"Mom and Blanche made biscuits, and I'm sure we have strawberry jam. I'll use the other camp stove to grill biscuits."

After Andy and Red woke, Red asked, "Where's Angel?"

"She's listening to the radio in the truck."

While Red hurried toward the truck, Jack said, "Send Annie here for breakfast; she can switch off with you then Angel, so y'all will have a hot breakfast too."

When Annie came to the picnic table, she said, "We haven't heard from Gabe yet, but from what the early-bird hams are saying, the second battalion didn't go much farther after dark last night; Angel said that was good. I'll probably replace her after I eat because she thinks Gabe won't be on the radio until after sunrise, but Angel told me to bring a snack for Red."

Andy sliced a small piece of ham for Red, then Stuart handed him a grilled biscuit.

Annie said, "Red told me she didn't know why, but the latest ham that Mama Sandra cured is the best she's ever had; she'll love the snack."

"I'll take it to her," Andy said. "Sit down and enjoy your breakfast."

Jack joined Annie at the table; while they ate, he asked, "How did you sleep?"

"I must have slept just fine because I closed my eyes, then Angel turned on the radio," Annie said.

"That's good; I think all of us were tired because as far as I know, nobody was restless at all last night."

When Andy returned, Stuart asked, "Did Angel wake you, or did you wake up and take over watch?"

"I woke up; she told me I was a little early, but I told her I was awake and couldn't go back to sleep, so she climbed into her sleeping bag and was out almost right away. I let Red sleep as long as I dared, then when she stirred, I tapped her shoulder and told her it was her turn."

Jack chuckled. "She was suspicious when I woke up and wanted to argue, but I guess she decided it wasn't wise to wake everyone else, so she slid into her sleeping bag and complained that it was cold and I was mean then went right to sleep."

"She has a point there, as far as climbing into a sleeping bag," Andy said. "I'm not about to tell her tomorrow will be worse, though."

After Angel joined them and she and Stuart ate, Angel said, "Gabe confirmed that bat two stopped not too long after dark. He wondered if they are planning to attack bat one tonight, but he didn't think we could count on it. The bat one leader has been on simplex most of this morning, and battalion one hasn't moved. He's still trying to reach the commander for an order to tell him whether to go west or south. Gabe wants to know which would be our preference. I think he's planning on intervening as the commander."

"If we tell them to go south for the rest of the day before they turn west tomorrow, will that work?" Andy asked.

"That should put them either a little north or a little south of us at nightfall, and if bat two is planning to attack them late tonight, bat two will be within striking distance," Angel said.

"Why are we intervening then? Why don't we just let them fight it out?" Andy asked.

Jack rubbed his chin. "I think I'm starting to catch on; we want bat one to be prepared for a fight, so bat two doesn't wipe them out then head straight for Doc Grayson."

"Right, but even if bat one is ready, bat two will wipe them out then continue toward their target," Andy said.

Stuart watched as Angel shook her head then returned to the truck. *What are we missing?*

CHAPTER EIGHT

Stuart bit his lip in thought then exhaled. *I think I know.* "We're taking one of each of the battalion's trucks. Bat two may have an advantage over bat one, which will be unable to continue at the same rate they have been because they'll be short on supplies. We need to ask Angel whether the militia will sweep in and clean up."

"Why didn't she tell us?" Andy asked.

"She told Gabe about our plan then told me that Gabe wants to help stop both battalions. What's the best way to stop both of them?"

"Turn them against each other, take away half their supplies, and follow up with a surprise attack," Jack said. "Angel really is a genius, isn't she?"

"Yes," Andy said with reverence in his tone.

"So, what do we do now? Just sit around?" asked Jack.

"Can you imagine us doing that? Like Red said, we'd be bored. We need to be familiar with the interstate to the north and south of us, so we'll be ready wherever bat one stops, and it wouldn't hurt to extend our familiarity to north ten miles from us for bat two," Stuart said.

"Annie and I can cover five miles north or south of us," Jack said.

Stuart nodded. "Andy, north or south?"

"Red and I will take the five miles south," Andy said.

"Angel and I can take the five miles north past Jack and Annie."

"We'll need to cover both sides of the interstate, right?" Jack asked.

"Yes, from what we know both of the battalions have set up on the east side of the southbound interstate so far, but there are no guarantees that they won't suddenly shift," Stuart said.

"We'll run all this past Angel, right?" Andy asked.

"Yes, but we'll have to pay attention and listen instead of our usual dashing off on a tangent." Jack shook his head. "Haven't we said that before?"

"Nope," said Andy.

"Not us; definitely not our style," Stuart said, then the three men laughed.

Red climbed out of the truck and glowered. "What's so funny?" she asked.

"I'll tell you after you have breakfast and a cup of hot tea," Andy said.

After Red and Andy ate, Stuart said, "Let's pack everything up. If Angel says it's time to move, we'll want to be ready."

Annie and Andy rolled up all the sleeping bags and folded the quilts while Stuart and Jack repacked the food into the truck then flipped the tarp to dry the side that had been on the ground. They left one camp stove out to make hot drinks.

Not long after they had cleaned up the camp, Angel joined them.

"Gabe pretended to be Old Jitters and growled the order to continue south," Angel said. "He didn't actually say he was Jitters, but everyone on the radio froze and didn't say anything for a few minutes; there was no questions about who it was. It was inspiring."

"Old Jitters Gabe has found his niche: impersonating bad guys," Jack said.

Annie opened the truck door. "Angel, you have to hear this. Gabe announced that Thursday is Christmas, and the hams are going wild discussing their plans. I think I heard Mr. Young ask for the best way to smoke a turkey."

"Perfect," Angel said before she joined Annie and Red in the truck.

"Why is that perfect?" Andy furrowed his brow then smiled. "Oh, I get it: the Christmas chatter is monopolizing the amateur radio communication channels; Gabe just jammed the radio waves."

"Are you sure? How did Gabe know?" Jack asked.

"Ready for this? Annie told me that she told Willa, so Willa must have told Gabe, who is smart enough to spot an advantage when he sees one." Stuart smiled.

Jack chuckled. "Let's look at the map again. I'd like to be better oriented on where we are."

Stuart spread out the map on the picnic table, and Angel joined them.

"We're here." Angel pointed to the map. "We need to consider our exit strategy and where Jack and Annie will stage."

Jack said, "It wouldn't hurt to have two options: one to travel west then south, and another one to travel southwest then west."

Andy pointed. "If we're going west, here is a road about three or four miles north of us; to go southwest, this road is about four or five miles south of us."

"Both of them go through small towns, which may be problematic, but if our lead truck is one of the transport trucks, that may help," Stuart said.

"If we go south then southwest, we could potentially pass near bat one, but if we go north to go west, we could travel too close to bat two; it depends on where the two battalions stop at the end of the day," Angel said.

"I'm going to grab Annie and head north; I'll take a handheld and be on our alternate simplex," Jack said. "We'll check out the road north of us that goes west, if you'll pick up from where we divert."

"We will." Stuart switched his handheld radio to their alternate simplex channel.

Jack and Annie refilled their canteens, picked up extra ammunition, and at Andy's urging, stuck a few snacks into their backpacks, then left.

"Red will be proud of you for making Annie take a snack; be sure to get full credit for that, Andy," Stuart said.

"Exactly what I had in mind." Andy smiled. "One team away from our base at a time makes sense to me. If Jack and Annie run into trouble, two of us can rush to assist while the other two protect our supplies."

"When they get back, we'll take a little time for a debriefing, probably over lunch, then you and Red can go south," Stuart said.

Angel and Red climbed out of the truck; Angel had her handheld on her hip and an earbud in her ear.

"Gabe and Angel agreed to monitor a simplex channel. The main channels are nonstop talk about Christmas," Red said. "If Gabe hears anything new, he'll give Angel a shout."

"I'd like to spend a little more time on the map," Stuart said.

Red glanced at Angel then Andy. "I'll grab a snack, then we'll all join you."

While the four of them studied the map, Stuart's radio crackled, and he turned up the volume.

"Abandoned..." the rest of Jack's traffic was broken up.

Stuart hopped into the truck bed then listened.

"Go for it," Stuart said.

After Stuart climbed down, he said, "They found an abandoned house a few miles down the road that goes west; the old house had been ransacked, and Jack said it looked like squatters had been there but not recently. The small barn behind the house had a new padlock on it, so they broke in and found a two-person utility task vehicle like number 48 and a trunk with rifles and ammunition. Jack thinks it's a stash for some bad guys, so they're bringing the trunk here. If we have time, Jack would like to take the UTV and the trunk to Gabe this afternoon."

"Red and I could take the pirates' booty to Gabe after lunch when we check the road to the south. We wouldn't be running any farther than we would have if we'd run our assignment and back."

Stuart nodded. "Fine with me. Angel can let Gabe know before you leave."

Angel snatched up her rifle then ran toward the lane and Stuart raced to catch up with her.

* * *

"She heard the UTV." Red munched on a strawberry scone and sipped her water.

Andy sat next to her at the picnic table and put his arm around her. "Did you hear it, honey?"

"Of course, I did..." Red's mouth quivered as she tried to hold back a smile. "...after Angel dashed to the lane."

"Should we be monitoring the radio?" Andy asked.

"Only if you need a recipe for sweet potato pie or cranberry compote, whatever that is. It's funny because Christmas was just another day for me when I was growing up. I didn't realize until after Mom died that she had been suffering for years; now I'm certain she must have loved Christmas before she became so sick."

"Christmas was a big deal at my house; do you understand why everyone is so excited about snow for Christmas?"

"Not really; I lived my whole life in Florida until Angel and I came with Stuart to help his folks. I've never seen snow in person, but it looks cold, and I'm not a fan of being cold."

"I'm looking forward to being with you when you see your first snow; it's magical, and we're lucky because we're kids, or did you forget?"

Red bit her lip then gazed at him. "What if it doesn't snow?"

"Then Blanche will have a story for us that explains who needed the snow more than we did."

Red leaned against him and sighed. "I love you even when you drive me crazy."

Andy kissed her forehead. "I know."

* * *

When they reached the end of the lane, Stuart asked, "Do you still hear the UTV?"

"No, something's wrong." She raced north on the shoulder, and Stuart followed her. When she neared the west-bound road, she jumped the ditch and crouched in the high grass; Stuart copied her every move and landed in the grass next to her.

"They aren't on the road. Key your radio," Angel whispered.

"Did you hear that? They're close," Angel said. "Whistle your cardinal call then follow me."

After Stuart whistled, a barred owl called out its signature 'who-cooks-for-you'. Angel paused then hooted the response, 'who-cooks-for-you-all.'

Stuart pointed to his radio when he heard the sound of a single squelch, then Angel quickly crept to the woods before she ran west.

Stuart scanned the trees and listened. *I don't see or hear her. I should have been ready to move.*

Stuart examined the brush and leaves but didn't see any broken stems on the brush or crushed leaves. As he cautiously made his way west through the woods, the forest thickened, and he slowed his pace. *I'm not even certain I'm still going west.*

He stopped and listened. *Nothing.*

Stuart adjusted his direction slightly to his right then continued as quietly as he could. Angel suddenly appeared next to him and motioned for him to follow her. *I didn't hear her coming.*

As he followed her, the crack of a rifle then a second crack ripped through the quiet forest, and the nearby small birds took flight.

Angel froze, and Stuart clicked the push-to-talk button once on his handheld then held his breath while he watched every muscle in Angel's body tense. When they heard Jack's two-click response, Angel relaxed, and Stuart exhaled in relief.

"What did you do that for?" A man screeched. "You killed both of them. Shot 'em right in the back."

Angel quietly lay prone in the grass and held her rifle ready to fire; Stuart took the same position next to her.

"Think about it," a second man growled. "We were responsible for hiding the stash of rifles and ammo in a safe place. When we got here, it was gone; those two goons ran ahead of us after we left camp, so they musta took off with it before we got here."

"Do you think anybody heard the shots?" the first man asked.

"Course not," the second man said. "We're miles from camp. Come on, let's head back before somebody thinks we know where those punks went with the rifles."

When they neared the intersection, the first man asked, "Are you sure they ran ahead and left us? I don't remember anything like that."

"You got a bad memory, fella."

A sharp crack startled the nearby crows that repeatedly cawed their warning as they flew en masse out of the trees.

Stuart listened intently to the sound of heavy footsteps as they headed to the east then faded away. *He must be running back to camp.*

He glanced at Angel, who nodded.

As she continued to lead him through the forest, the trees thinned, and the forest brightened; Stuart sighed with relief when he spotted Jack through the trees.

After Stuart and Angel joined Jack and Annie, Jack said, "Annie heard a commotion on the road and drove across the ditch and into the trees. I thought she'd lost control for a second until I heard the men coming our way. I knew exactly when they reached the barn because they began blaming each other for leaving the barn unlocked."

Stuart raised his eyebrows. *When I was a deputy, I never knew my sheriff was accomplished at picking locks.*

Stuart rolled his eyes. *I'm wrong; Annie is accomplished with any tool she picks up. She could pick a lock faster than I could unlock a padlock with a key.*

"Give us a minute, and we'll check the road ahead of you," Stuart said. "I'll click once if it's clear, and three clicks if you need to hide."

"Twenty-seven clicks if we're in trouble." Annie beamed when Jack and Stuart chuckled.

"That was funny, Annie," Angel said.

Annie raised her eyebrows. "Thank you; you got the joke!"

When Stuart and Angel reached the intersection, Angel slowly scanned the trees across the road to the east while Stuart peered at the trees and listened. Angel pointed to a driveway north of them on the other side of the road; Stuart waited then heard a truck engine. He watched as the truck lumbered to the road then turned north and sped away.

When her foot twitched, Stuart clicked his handheld, then Angel took off toward their camp as the sound of the UTV headed their way; Stuart ran alongside her. *I was ready.*

When Angel sped up, Stuart pushed himself to stay with her. *Annie's trying to catch us; she and Angel are racing.* Stuart put his head down and focused on running as hard as he could. He slowed when they reached the turn to their lane, but Angel disappeared as she sped away.

Annie roared to the intersection then slowed for the turn and stopped next to Stuart. "Where's Angel?" she asked.

"Probably finishing up lunch and finalizing her plans to infiltrate bat one," Stuart said.

Jack smiled, and Annie said, "Not funny, Dad; it's probably true."

"I'll meet you at the camp in a few minutes," Stuart said. "I want to watch the road for a bit."

"You can take it from here, Annie." Jack climbed out to join Stuart.

As Annie sped away, Jack shook his head. "She picked up her love of a fierce competition from Red and Angel."

"At least she's learning from the best," Stuart said.

"What are we waiting for?" Jack asked.

"I needed a little time to think. Angel and I watched a truck as it came out of an overgrown driveway then headed north. I assume he's returning to bat one, but what makes him think his story will fly? Why not just take the truck and desert?"

The two men sat in silence, then Jack said, "He could be confident because he's higher in the ranks. He might have a cushy position and doesn't have to scrounge for food, shelter, or security."

"Do you think they have more rifle and ammo caches along the way?" Stuart asked.

"Maybe, but I don't understand why they'd want to do that with the transportation resources that they have unless there's a rogue who wants to take over bat one."

Stuart furrowed his brow. "Maybe the rogue works for bat two and has been diverting resources."

"If that's true, I'm even happier that Annie and I snatched the trunk."

"Andy suggested that he and Red take the UTV and trunk to Gabe after lunch when they check the road to the south. What do you think?" Stuart asked.

"I like it. I'd worry about overtaxing Red, but Andy, with Annie's backing, is doing a fine job of reining in our headstrong Dead Eye Red."

"Ready to head back?"

"Yep, for now, I don't see where we have any need to change our plans."

"We've had our lunch and are ready to leave," Andy said.

"Jack agreed with your idea of taking the trunk and UTV to Gabe," Stuart said. "Does it need gas?"

"It's full. We think the owners of the property left in a hurry and couldn't take the UTV with them. We would have drained the tank, but they must not have had time," Annie said. "I think it's strange that none of the squatters broke into the barn."

"City folks," Jack said.

Annie nodded.

"Gabe knows you're on your way, and I asked him about that rifle you love, and he said to keep it and the ammo for it," Angel said.

"Thanks, Angel," Red said.

"Show me which one, honey," Andy said.

After Andy removed the rifle, Stuart pulled out all the ammunition for it then closed the trunk.

Andy surveyed the stack of boxes of ammunition. "We wouldn't have been able to bring it all back; thanks from me too for asking Gabe, Angel."

Red grabbed her rifle and a handheld before she climbed into the UTV; after she was seated, Andy slowly drove down the lane.

"You drive like an old man," Red grumbled.

"Fine; you drive, and I'll shoot your rifle."

"You will not."

Stuart smiled and listened as Red tried to start arguments with Andy, who calmly deflected them all.

"Our lunch is ready," Angel said.

While they ate, Annie said, "I told Red about our one, two, four, and twenty-seven clicks. She'll break the squelch one time when they get to Gabe's. What do we do if we get an emergency call?"

"Good question, Annie. We'll stick with our plan: two stay here to protect our supplies, and two leave to rescue. If it's the four of us here, we'd send Stuart and Angel."

Annie nodded. "Logical, Dad. What if the four here are Red, Andy, you, and me?"

"You and I go."

"Red won't like that," she said.

"Just go," Angel said.

Jack's handheld squawked once, and he clicked twice to acknowledge.

* * *

After Andy parked in front of Gabe's house, Willa met them on the porch and hugged Red. "I'm so happy to see you again. Gabe's in his computer room and is anxious to talk to you two. If you can spend a little time with me before you leave, Mama made snacks for us."

"We have a trunk of rifles and ammunition for Gabe," Red said.

"Mama, if you would, please send my younger brothers out here to carry in a heavy trunk to Gabe's office," Willa called out.

When two large men came out of the house, Andy stood back and smiled.

"Thanks, man; Gabe's gonna love this." One of the young men picked up the trunk and carried it inside. The other brother, Willa, Red, and Andy followed him.

When the young man set down the trunk then opened it, Gabe's eyes widened. "Angel told me you had a box for me with a few things, but I definitely wasn't expecting rifles and ammunition; so you found a rifle you liked, Red?"

"It's a smaller deer rifle but not as small as a youth size; it's an absolutely perfect fit for me."

"Angel said there was some bling that was a perfect fit to go with your choice. Does that mean you found ammo for it too?"

"Sure did," she said.

"We brought you a UTV too. We can't take it with us and don't want to abandon it, either, so it's yours," Andy said.

"You just answered my next question because I couldn't imagine how you hauled that large trunk here," Gabe said. "Are you sure about the UTV?"

"Positive, you're doing us a favor. What do you have?" Andy asked.

Red sat on the chair next to Gabe's desk and pulled out her notebook from her backpack. "Ready to take notes."

Gabe nodded. "Your bat one seems to have become better organized. The hams think there was a coup, and they might be right because the spotters reported bat one has been training in squads since dawn; one ham reported his spotter called it a crash course in military basic training. Your bat two is about fifteen miles away, and they stopped for what most of the spotters called an extended break. One of the spotters expects the break to be brief, so bat two can be close enough late tonight, within two to five miles was his estimate, to strike bat one tomorrow before dawn."

"Is that it?" Red asked. "I'd like to spend a little time with Willa."

"That's it," Gabe said, and Red dashed out of the room.

"The spotter must be a teacher because only a teacher can read a quiet, resting crowd that is about to explode," Andy said.

Gabe splinted his side with a small pillow as he laughed. "Only a teacher would even think of it. What did you teach?"

"I've studied military history and tactics my entire life and love to work with my hands, so the private boys' school assigned me to teach physics. I turned the lab into a woodworking shop and was almost fired."

Gabe grabbed his pillow when he burst out laughing again. "So how well do these latest changes with bat one and bat two work with your plan?"

"We couldn't ask for anything better; all we have to do is pull it off, which reminds me, be prepared to defend your home and family against an onslaught sometime after dawn tomorrow. If our plan succeeds, you won't see anyone at all; if we fail, you're in the direct path between bat one and two and their target."

"Is it possible to get us word when you're successful?"

"I'm sure that's already in Angel's plan."

"She's amazing; always thinking, that one. Do you need any help? Willa's two younger brothers would be more than willing to help wherever they're needed."

"They're needed here," Andy said. "We're going to stir up two hornets' nests then run and hope they annihilate each other and never realize we were there, which reminds me, Red and I should probably head back. We've got more groundwork to do, and I'd like to get your information back to Angel and Stuart."

Gabe smiled. "Willa would say you should leave Red here with us, so she'll be safe, but I can't imagine Red anywhere other than in the middle of the action."

"You nailed it."

CHAPTER NINE

Stuart and Annie returned after their stealthy walk halfway up the lane and back.

"How's it going?" Jack looked up as Annie flounced to the picnic table where he was sharpening his knife.

"If stomping through the grass was stealthy, I'd be in great shape." Annie joined her dad. Stuart poured a cup of coffee before he sat.

Angel stepped out of the truck where she had been listening to the radio. "Gabe said his entire family has gathered for Christmas, and a rare redwing visited earlier but is gone now."

"That must mean that Willa's brothers arrived; with the extra rifles and ammunition, they'll be able to defend their family," Stuart said.

Angel returned to the radio.

"How long will it be until Red and Andy are here?" Annie asked.

"Assuming they went straight to Gabe's in the UTV, it may be a couple of hours before they return," Stuart said.

"Does that cut into your time to check the north past the five miles that Dad and I checked?" she asked.

"We'll be fine; we want to find the best way to approach bat one then continue to bat two, so we can leave Red and Andy at bat one while we go to bat two and steal a truck before Red and Andy take their truck. I want to see where all their trucks are parked and get a sense of their security. Let's go over that map again, Jack."

Jack pointed to a road that headed west that was south and west of bat one. "I've been thinking if we stage here, and you go east with the truck from bat two before you turn south, then Andy and Red can head southwest almost straight to us with their bat one truck."

Stuart furrowed his brow as he studied the map. "We need a second rendezvous point in case you have to move, or we can't make it to you."

Annie leaned closer to the map as she examined it.

"What are you thinking, Annie?" Jack asked.

"Could the second rendezvous point be on the way to get back to our families?"

"That definitely has possibilities if anyone is trying to follow us because they wouldn't expect us to backtrack by turning north," Stuart said. "While Angel and I are gone, maybe you could go over everything we've discussed with Red and Andy; they might have some ideas too."

Angel climbed out of the truck. "Are you ready to take over the radio while I check my backpack, Annie?"

After Annie climbed into the truck, Angel said, "We'll need warm coats tonight because the cold weather will hit us sooner than everyone thought. The two battalions are both using the same channel for simplex, but I'm not picking up anything yet, and according to the ham operators, they aren't close enough to hear each other. Mr. Young started a rumor of a militia at the Florida-Georgia state line heading north toward bat one, and the rumor was accepted as fact and has spread pretty quickly. The hams think bat one is looking for a place where they can dig in. The spotters reported that bat two has packed up and is ready to move. I didn't hear anything that would cause us to adjust our plans."

Angel and Stuart refilled their canteens and added ham biscuits to their backpacks then stuffed in their heavy coats.

Annie opened the truck door. "A man on the radio just said, 'Militia confirmed.' Maybe it's someone who is working with Mr. Young, but no one responded; I'll let you know if I hear anything else."

"She's probably right about one of Mr. Young's cohorts," Jack said.

Stuart nodded. "Angel, we have straps to attach our sleeping bags to our backpacks. Would that add too much weight if we need to run?"

"The extra bulk of the sleeping bags would make it more difficult to go through the brush and trees without being seen or heard," Angel said. "If we're separated from the others and don't have a truck to sleep in, we'll build a small shelter and snuggle to stay warm."

Stuart hugged her. "You're so smart."

"Red and Andy are close." Angel wiggled, and Stuart released her but was ready to run alongside her when she dashed to the lane.

"Everything okay?" Stuart asked when they met Red and Andy.

"We're fine," Andy said. "Let's take a break, and we'll catch you up."

"Hot tea or water?" Angel asked.

Red put on her sweatshirt. "Hot tea, please; it's getting chilly, isn't it?"

"Annie told us to save the goat cheese for you, Red. Do you want crackers or a ham biscuit to go with that?" Jack asked.

"Ham biscuit."

After Andy and Red sat at the picnic table, Andy said, "Gabe and Willa's brothers appreciated the rifles and ammunition. They'll be able to protect their family if any deserters show up at Gabe's house. Gabe tried to turn down the UTV, but I convinced him that there was no way we could take it with us."

Red pinched off a small bite of biscuit then tore a sliver of ham and ate them together. "We believe we saw two scouts from bat one. They were walking south in the middle of the northbound interstate road, and while we watched, one of them grabbed the other one's arm and whispered, then the other guy pulled out his handheld from its holder and spoke into it before they abruptly turned north and broke into a fast run."

"We thought something had scared them until we heard the guy on the radio say, 'Militia confirmed'. Did you hear them? They weren't on simplex. At first I thought they'd seen us and thought we were the militia, but they didn't turn back until after they passed us, and even redbird was well hidden." Andy grinned.

"We were curious, so we headed south for a mile or so and didn't see or hear anything. Gabe told us about Mr. Young's rumor about the militia. I think they were afraid to go any farther in case they did actually run into them, so they just confirmed."

Jack chuckled. "Don't you know Mr. Young was proud of himself when he heard them on the radio? Do you think they'll blame the militia or bat two when you steal one of their trucks? I'll tell Annie about the scouts after we finalize our plans."

"We expect bat one to set up their camp within five miles of us, and we think bat two will be less than five miles north of bat one; it sounds like bat two still plans to attack bat one just before dawn," Angel said.

"We'll check this afternoon for the best route for us to take, then the four of us will leave sometime after midnight. Our current plan is that we'll leave you near the bat one truck then run to the bat two truck and steal it. When you think we've had enough time to take our truck, then you take your truck. Jack can go over the routes on the map with you," Stuart said. "That's it, so far; we'll finalize our plans after Angel and I get back."

As Angel and Stuart ran at Stuart's comfortable pace, he asked, "Should we stay on this side of the interstate to find bat one and bat two?"

"Yes, no one would be between us and the camp if there is any trouble."

After a few miles, Angel slowed and whispered, "I hear voices ahead." She led the way into the trees, and they continued.

After Stuart heard the voices too, he nodded.

Angel slowed then stopped. "They are just ahead, and it sounds like they are moving to the other side of the interstate. Let's take a peek then take a break."

When they reached the edge of the trees, they commando crawled their way through the high grass and weeds.

Stuart narrowed his eyes then counted the men. *Eighteen.*

He and Angel watched as a driver and a passenger climbed into each truck, then four men led the way for the first truck to follow over the median to the other side of the interstate. The rest of the men milled around in small groups until one of the four men shouted for them to follow the trucks.

"No one is on guard," Stuart whispered.

The drivers parked the trucks next to each other facing south on the northbound travel lanes.

A man shouted, "Get the tents set up."

Four men shuffled to the truck that had parked close to the field on the other side of the highway; the driver climbed out of the truck and lifted the rear rolling door then tossed the keys to a man and strolled to a smaller tent. The man with the truck keys took the keys to the driver's side and dropped them inside.

The two passengers hopped inside the back and slid the large, rolled tent canvas, the bundle of tent stakes, and two stacks of folded cots toward the edge of the truck.

Two men carried the canvas, and two men carried the stakes to the field. The driver barked an order, and three more men trudged to help put up the tent while the two men in the back of the truck slid a large, portable grill, a propane cooktop, and a large box to the edge to be unloaded.

"If they've unloaded food and their shelter I'll bet they don't unload the truck that is closer to us," Stuart whispered. "That's our target truck for Red and Andy to take. They can drive it over the median at the same place then head south and take an exit."

"If the other truck still has its keys in it, Andy will take its keys too," Angel said.

"Let's find the other battalion."

They crawled backward until they were out of sight then hurried through the trees.

Angel paused. "Men's voices."

She continued at a slow pace, and Stuart tried to walk as quietly as she did.

"Here," Angel said.

They commando crawled to the edge of the tall grass; Stuart peered at the interstate then lowered his head. "Their camp is in a field across from the northbound lane, just like bat one; they have almost finished setting up a large tent and a smaller tent with a grill and burners. I'd estimate there are forty men. No one is idle, but I don't see anyone standing guard. They left one truck on the southbound side."

"I may have to hotwire it to get it going."

She raised her head high enough to examine the group then lowered it. "They are highly trained, disciplined, and won't deviate from their plan. Their leader may be arrogant, which explains why there is no one on guard duty."

"That's interesting; do you think they'll react quickly when we take the truck?"

"They didn't position their truck in the northbound lane very well for a rapid response, but that doesn't mean they couldn't. We'll just have to grab and go. We'll need to look at the map with Jack to see what we should do because going east might be difficult unless we take their northbound truck, but that seems foolhardy."

"Yes." Stuart smirked, and Angel elbowed him.

My cloud told her.

Stuart and Angel jumped over snags and weaved past the trees as they ran back through the woods. When Angel stopped to listen, Stuart listened too. *I don't hear anyone talking, but she might. I'm not sure I ever understood what an asset her sensitive hearing would be.*

"We can run now," Angel said, and they raced back to camp.

When they reached their campsite, Andy and Jack met them, and Annie waved from the truck.

"Red's taking a nap; she agreed to relax only after I promised her I'd wake her when you showed up." Andy left then returned with Red.

"Both groups emptied one truck but not the other and have settled in; three of the trucks are in the northbound side of the interstate, and both of your trucks are facing south. The crossover to the southbound side for your truck is relatively level, so you can travel south on the interstate and take your exit. The truck that we plan to take is on the southbound side of the interstate and is facing south. We need to decide where we exit because going south is our only option," Stuart said.

"Our original thought was that different directions would scatter the pursuit teams," Angel said, "but maybe we'd have the advantage of safety in numbers because the two battalions are more likely to clash when they meet."

Andy furrowed his brow. "The timing becomes more critical because if we take our truck first, we don't want you to run up on the bat one team chasing us, and if you take your truck first, we don't want to run into the bat two team when we cross over to the southbound lane."

Jack pointed to the map. "Andy, if you take this first exit, and Angel, if you take the second or third exit, then any pursuit team will have to make a choice. The timing's still critical, though."

Stuart rubbed his face. "Maybe less than we're thinking because we're assuming both teams will immediately jump to their second truck with a pursuit team as soon as they hear the engines start. Andy, bat one's driver of the truck you're not taking tossed the keys to another man; his assignment must have been to make sure their equipment arrived safely, and that's all."

"It may take them a little time to gather a team; did you see anyone with a sidearm or carrying a rifle?" Jack asked.

"There were two men with sidearms at bat two, but no one carried a rifle; I didn't see rifles at either camp, but they hadn't finished unloading," Angel said.

Red smiled. "The leadership must not trust their troops at all. If we're lucky, all their firearms and ammunition are in the trucks we're stealing."

"Our original plan was for you to give us enough time to get to bat two then grab your truck, and we can coordinate that with our handhelds," Stuart said. "If either of us has trouble accessing our truck or getting it started, we should abandon the truck and get away as fast as we can."

"Where do we go?" Andy asked.

"Gabe's," Angel and Red said in unison.

Jack chuckled. "I think we're pulling together a pretty good plan, so where would we want our back up meeting place to be if the first one falls through for anyone? Annie suggested we select somewhere that is on the way back to our families' farms." Jack pointed to a small town. "How about here?"

"Would it make sense if we make it our primary since Stuart and Angel aren't coming from the east anymore?" Andy asked.

"Yes."

"Our new primary meeting point isn't too far from the farms. If it isn't safe, Annie will let you know, and we can meet halfway between there and home," Jack said.

"I'll relieve Annie." Angel hurried to the white pickup.

"After I refill our tank, I'll get a pot of coffee going and heat up some water for hot tea." Jack refolded the map then rose from the table.

As sunset neared, Stuart strode to the crate where they had stored the food, and Andy followed him.

"I thought we deserved a hot meal; I'm sure both Mom and Molly packed something we can heat up."

"Here are three quarts of canned stew from Molly, probably venison that Annie harvested, and here's some flat bread from Blanche; I think we're set," Andy said.

"Mom packed peach cobbler. I think I can steam-heat this while we eat," Stuart said.

While Andy heated the stew, Jack made two cups of hot tea.

"Andy, would you join Red and Annie while they eat first, so they can replace Angel on the radio?" Stuart asked.

"I can do that, then I'll take care of steaming the dessert," Andy said. "The stew is ready when we are."

Red and Annie put their mess bowls on the picnic table next to their hot tea while Stuart heated their fry bread in the skillet. Andy scooped hot stew into the three bowls then joined Red and Annie at the table.

"This looks delicious; thank you for the small portion, honey." Red sipped her hot tea then dipped a piece of her fry bread into the stew.

After they ate, Red replaced Angel.

"I contacted Gabe and told him we were looking forward to roast beef," Angel said.

"Excellent," Stuart said.

Jack, Andy, and Annie took down their tent then rolled it up and loaded it into the back of the truck while Stuart and Angel cleaned then packed their cooking pans and utensils and dishes.

"We should sleep in two shifts, so we can cover the radio and our security," Angel said.

"Andy, Red, and I will take the first shift," Jack said, and Andy nodded.

"I'd like to walk to the end of the lane," Jack said.

Something's on Jack's mind. "I'll go with you."

Stuart and Jack picked up their rifles then headed toward the road.

"I'm worried about Red," Jack said. "She's doing fine, but I'm not sure she would have the energy to make it to Gabe's, especially after being shorted sleep. I've considered suggesting that Annie and I switch places with them, but Annie's not as fast or experienced as Red."

"It might be a good idea if the four of us put lightweight food in our backpacks, so we'll have the snacks for a quick refuel on the way to our rendezvous point or to Gabe's. I'll talk to Andy."

"I'm sure Annie will give Red a snack before we leave too."

When they reached the interstate, Jack chuckled. "I'm surprised anyone has any fuel at all; the only reason we do is because we have an Angel who never lets our supply run low."

"Her specialty." Stuart gazed at the sky. "The moon's bright, but the clouds are rolling in; we'll have enough light to see after midnight, but we won't be in the spotlight of a bright moon."

When they returned, Stuart said, "Mom said she put lightweight snacks in for us. I'm sure we'll eat a little something before we leave, but we need to carry snacks with us if we need them to get us to Gabe's."

"Let's see what we have, and I'll pack Red's too." Andy grinned. "Cuts down on the extra discussion."

"Angel, we're packing snacks into our backpacks," Stuart said.

Angel brought her backpack to the food crate. "Can we come close to what Mama Sandra packed for us? Tell Andy she gave Red extra protein."

After Andy loaded his and Red's backpacks with as many snacks as he dared, he asked Jack, "Are we ready for our power nap? What are you giving us, Stuart? Two or three hours?"

"I'll try for three; four if I can squeeze it in."

"I'll tell Red it's time for her power nap," Angel said.

Red stormed out of the truck. "Angel told me I'm on the first shift to sleep tonight. Who's bright idea was that?"

"Mine," Jack said. "You, Andy, and I are the first shift."

Red gaped at where the tent had stood. "No tent?"

"We want to get up and leave," Andy said.

"I'm going to freeze," Red grumbled.

"No, you won't. I've already zipped our sleeping bags together," Andy said.

"Well, that's not fair; I'll listen to your breathing and fall right to sleep." Red put her hands on her hips, and Annie giggled.

"Don't encourage him." Red smiled.

"Let's have a bedtime snack, Red. I have a special treat for us. Cookie sandwiches with goat cheese for the filling; it's my personal creation.

I found some goat cheese that Mom had hidden in my backpack just for you and me."

"I love Aunt Molly; she's the best." Red linked her arm with Annie's, and the two of them strolled to the picnic table then enjoyed their snack.

"Your new creation was yummy, Annie; thank you." Red hugged her then rose from the table. "Come on, Andy; the sooner I fall asleep, the sooner we get to leave."

"I can't argue with logic like that," Andy said.

* * *

When Red woke, Andy was disentangling from her and trying to slip out of the sleeping bag. "I'm awake too," she said.

Red and Andy rolled up their sleeping bags while Jack waited at the back of the truck to load it.

"All loaded? Be safe." Jack and Annie climbed into the truck, and he headed down the lane with his headlights off.

"Let's go," Angel said.

"You lead, Angel, but don't leave us behind," Stuart said.

When they neared bat one's location, Angel ducked low and walked through the high grass; Stuart, Red, and Andy followed her in single file.

When they peered at the camp, Red exhaled. *No movement; no signs of any guards.*

"One click, success; two clicks, acknowledge; three clicks, on the way to Gabe's," Andy whispered.

"Twenty-seven clicks, help," Red added, and everyone nodded, then Angel and Stuart disappeared into the grass.

"Ready, honey?" Andy asked.

"For Peyton: Hell, yeah," she whispered.

"You lead, but don't leave me because I have to be quiet too," Andy said.

Red raced to the interstate then continued to the median; she lay flat in the grass and waited while Andy made his way as quietly and quickly as he could. When he joined her, Red dashed across to their truck and stood close to the truck near the back tires.

Andy hurried to join her. Red followed him as he rounded the front of the truck then stood guard while he opened the driver's door, picked up the keys on the floor board and climbed in but didn't shut his door. Red raced around the truck then climbed into the passenger's seat and held onto her door.

"We'll slam our doors when the engine starts," Andy whispered, and Red nodded.

When he turned the key, he glanced at the gauges and moaned. "We're in trouble."

"What's wrong?" Red whispered.

"No gas."

"Give it a try anyway; maybe the gauge is broken," Red hissed.

When the engine started, they slammed their doors as Andy accelerated the truck to cross the median. Red clicked her handheld push-to-talk button once, and immediately heard the two-click response followed by a single click. She responded with two.

After they were in the southbound lane, Red narrowed her eyes as he pushed the accelerator to the floor, and the engine coughed and sputtered.

Andy slowed and drove across the ditch to the frontage road then headed toward their camp; after he turned at the lane and traveled a few yards, the engine coughed, and the truck lurched forward then stopped.

Red gazed at the sky that had turned from dark black to dark blue with the sliver of daylight on the horizon. *Mom told me this is the blue hour sky before she was sick.*

Red furrowed her brow as she listened. *Still haven't heard a truck following us.*

When she heard a truck as it sped south on the interstate, she exhaled. *I'll bet that's Stuart and Angel.*

"What now?" she asked.

"I don't think we can be seen from the road, what do you think?"

They crept to the end of the lane and listened to the shouts from the bat one camp.

They were almost at the end of the lane when Andy whispered, "I see the truck. They would have to come this far before they could see it."

"What do we do?" Red asked.

"Let's check the back of the truck then head to Gabe's while they're in complete chaos," Andy said.

Andy removed the open padlock then opened the roll-up back door and whistled. "Look at all that firepower. I'll lock up the truck."

He set the padlock on the bumper then locked the doors to the cab.

"This padlock that was on there had a key in the lock. I tried it and it unlocks the padlock," Red said.

"We'll use that to lock up the back. I'll add it to the truck key ring."

"Let's go," Red said as Andy struggled with getting the small key onto the large keyring. "Just give it to me or put it in your pocket."

"I'll give you the truck keys and the padlock key, so they'll be together. Did you click to let Stuart and Angel know we're going to Gabe's?"

"Sure did."

"Why don't I carry the handheld? That's one less thing to slow you down."

Red rolled her eyes. *Definitely overprotective; we'll argue later.*

She gave him the handheld then reached to put the keys in her pocket and frowned. "I'd rather hide them close to the truck, then any of us can move it."

She furrowed her brow as she scanned the area. *Picnic table.* "Lift one side of the picnic table, and I'll clear a little hole for the keys."

After Andy lifted the heavy table, Red deepened the impression in the dirt where one leg had settled then dropped the keys into the deeper impression and covered the keys with the dirt she had removed.

"Okay, down."

They examined the leg and the dirt around it, then Andy tried to rock the still-stable table.

"Good enough; let's go," Red said.

When they reached the end of the lane, Andy pushed Red behind him then pulled her close and whispered, "Four men walking the interstate going south; I think they're searching for any tracks. They must have found where we crossed to the frontage road."

"We need to get away from the truck."

"Let's go to the woods, then we can move faster. We need to get to Gabe's before they do, if they're going that far south."

Before they reached the woods, Andy and Red heard nearby shots; they immediately dropped to the ground in the brush and weeds. Red listened for a few more minutes. "It's all north of us, let's go."

She led the way to the woods as the sky lightened from dark to light blue when shots rang out. Andy grunted and dropped to the ground. Red's eyes widened as the red stain on the shoulder of his shirt spread. She dragged him deeper into the tall grass then crept back to where she heard the shot when everything went black.

CHAPTER TEN

Sandra woke with a start when she heard a cry coming from the boys' room upstairs. She threw on her robe, and Scott mumbled, "Is something wrong?"

"Henry's having a nightmare. Go back to sleep."

She dashed up the stairs; Henry was standing next to the window as he screamed, "Mama Angel, find Red. We have to find Red."

Brandon stood next to Henry as he awkwardly patted Henry's back. Jimmy huddled in his bed and chewed on his blanket.

Sandra grabbed both boys in a hug. "Shhh, shhh. You're okay, Henry. Mama Angel will find Red for us. Shhh, shhh."

Henry relaxed then Sandra led him back to bed. "Go back to sleep boys; it's too early to get up, and Red is okay because Mama Angel will find her."

"Yes, Mama Angel will find Red," Henry mumbled, and all three boys snuggled under their covers.

Sandra tiptoed down the stairs. *Kitchen lantern's on. Bless her, Blanche is starting our coffee.*

Sandra went into the kitchen. "Henry had another nightmare. They certainly must be vivid. This time he was shouting for Mama Angel to find Red, and Brandon was trying to comfort him; the nightmares scare poor Jimmy, and I don't say that I blame him. The boys are asleep now. I'll throw on some clothes, thanks for making coffee."

"It's what a good chuckwagon cook does while the trail boss takes care of the cowhands." Blanche winked.

Sandra chuckled as she hurried to dress in the dark. When she returned to the kitchen, Blanche had poured two cups of coffee.

Sandra joined Blanche at the table and wrapped her hands around her cup for warmth. "After my second cup, I'll start a fire in the fireplace. It turned downright cold overnight didn't it?"

"Not unexpected." Blanche sipped her coffee. "In yesterday's nightmare, Henry warned Mama Angel to hide because they might see her. Today's nightmare, he wants Mama Angel to find Red, and it almost sounds like Mama Angel doesn't know that Red needs to be found to me."

"Are you thinking we're getting up-to-date status of what's going on from Henry?" Sandra asked. "I know he's really stressed about Angel and Stuart being gone, but his nightmares are so specific."

"Could be or maybe we're getting an in-depth idea of what worries Henry."

Sandra nodded and refilled their cups. "Tomorrow's Christmas Eve. David wants to know if we want the Christmas tree set up here in the kitchen or in the living room."

Ethel, Doc Larkin's old black dog with a gray muzzle, rose from her favorite location near the stove and padded to the back door.

"You ready to join those rascals outside, Ethel?" Blanche opened the door, and Ethel trotted outside. Blanche dished up food for the three dogs into their bowls.

When a dog scratched on the back door, Sandra opened the door, and the pups, Brody and Tracker, bounded inside followed by the more refined Ethel. Brody and Tracker were brothers and looked like their yellow lab father, but had the markings of their collie mother, Holly, who lived with Andy's Uncle Leo.

Brody and Tracker scrambled to Blanche and stood in front of her until she held up their bowls. "Sit." The two pups dropped into a sit and watched Blanche as she put the bowls in front of them then pointed as she said, "Okay."

The boys dug in and Ethel padded to the other side of Blanche and sat as Blanche placed her bowl in front of her. "Good girl."

Ethel ate daintily and much slower than the two pups who had already finished their breakfasts and were licking each other's bowls for any miniscule scraps that their brother missed.

"I don't know about you, but I can handle only so many dogs, buckeroos, and busybody men in the kitchen at one time. Why don't we tell David to set up the tree in the living room?"

Sandra chuckled. "I've got the perfect spot; I'll show him when he wanders in for coffee."

After Sandra started the fire in the fireplace, she moved an overstuffed chair, a table, and a lamp to make room for the tree in the corner near the front door then pushed the sofa farther away from the corner. She moved another table to make room for the overstuffed chair then crowded the first table next to the chair.

She stood back and examined the room. "It'll do."

She carried the lamp with her when she returned to the kitchen.

Blanche glanced up from the stove. "Taking your lamp for a walk?"

"It's been sitting in the same place in the living room for so long, that I wasn't seeing it anymore. I could be an optimist and ask Stuart to put it in the attic for me, but that doesn't make any sense. I don't know what to do with it."

Blanche chuckled. "You'll figure it out. The buckeroos want to make Christmas presents for their parents today. Any ideas?"

"I have a bunch of warm knit caps in different colors, don't ask why; the kids could create designs in felt then glue them onto the caps."

"That's an awesome idea. How many do you have?"

Sandra felt her face grow warm. "I think about fifty."

Blanche nodded.

She doesn't want to embarrass me.

"Shall we share with the other families?" Blanche asked. "Do we have enough felt?"

"I love the idea of sharing; I'll have to check on the felt. When Noel comes to get his coffee to take to the radio, I'll ask him to mention them to Mr. Young."

"Do you have any ideas how you will send the caps to Lela? I'm sure she'll want to manage their projects," Blanche said.

"Hand it off to Scott; that's a project right up his alley."

"It certainly would be, but we don't want to pull away all our security from the house. Louisa and I could go, or another option we have is Mandy; Noel and I have been working on Mandy's shooting skills, so Mandy and I could go."

"Mandy? She's only ten years old," Sandra said.

"Don't make me pull my Indignant Old Woman card. How old was Stuart the first time he went hunting with his dad?"

"Touché." Sandra rolled her eyes.

"Let's talk to Louisa."

"Talk to Louisa about what?" Louisa hurried into the kitchen and headed to the coffee pot.

"This first part is top secret, so you'll have to erase it from your mind." Blanche told Louisa about the knit caps and the felt decorations.

"Mind erased." Louisa sipped her coffee.

Blanche nodded. "Well done. We have some items we'd like to take to Lela for the Mitchell, Cabello, and Starr children, and one option is that Mandy and I take the items."

"That's interesting; I'm sure you considered you and me going, but it's a short, relatively safe trip and a great opportunity for Mandy to gain some confidence as a member of the team," Louisa said.

"Exactly what I thought; she's ready for that next step of being trusted with being responsible for herself and a team member," Blanche said.

"What do you think, Sandra?" Louisa asked.

"I think you would be too young to go." Sandra smiled.

Louisa laughed. "I understand completely. I'll always worry about Mandy and Jimmy even after they are adults, won't I?"

"I do have a serious question," Sandra said. "Will Ethan feel left out?"

"No," Louisa said. "David has already asked Ethan to help him with the Christmas tree; even if Ethan wasn't going to be busy, I think it's important for all of the children to learn that not being included in one assignment doesn't mean that they are not valued members of the family."

"You have got to be the best mom in the world, and I'm serious," Sandra said.

Louisa blushed. "Thank you."

Sandra smiled then rose to make another pot of coffee. "What's on the menu this morning, chuckwagon chef?"

"What about pancakes and bacon?" Blanche hurried to put on her apron.

"If you'll mix the batter, I'll fry the bacon," Sandra said.

"What's the lesson for this morning, Blanche?" Louisa asked. "Is there anything I can do to prepare in advance?"

"I planned to talk about weather conditions and different types of precipitation. Do you know how to make fog in a bottle?"

"I actually do," Louisa smiled. "So we'll talk about fog and the temperature differences then move on to rain, freezing rain, sleet, and snow. Do you have a book with pictures or graphics of the different precipitations?"

"Sure do; I'll fetch it for you right after breakfast."

When Mandy, who had her mother's dark skin, and Aria came down the stairs together and into the kitchen, Sandra smiled.

Aria raised her arms and twirled to show off her long-sleeved pale green T-shirt with a sequined Christmas tree on the front. "Mandy found Christmas shirts for me, and I picked this one. I like Christmas shirts. Is today Christmas?"

"No, honey. Christmas is in two more days," Louisa said.

"Two days is a very long time, Mama." Aria sighed as she sat in her chair that was next to Mandy's.

"We have to set the table, Aria," Mandy said.

"Oh, yes; I forgot."

"We'll need forks, knives, butter, syrup, and strawberry jam. We'll let your mama pour the milk," Sandra said.

Mandy and Aria washed their hands, then Mandy handed the forks and knives to Aria, who carefully placed a set at each plate while Mandy set the butter, syrup, and strawberry jam on the table. Mandy added a spoon next to the jam, then she put her hands on her hips and asked, "Have we forgotten anything, Mom?"

Louise smiled as she glanced at the table. "Looks like you've gotten everything; good job."

Mandy held up her hand, and Aria smacked a high five, then the two girls took their seats.

While Louisa poured two glasses of milk, and Blanche poured the pancake batter on her hot griddle, Scott, Cal, and David came into the kitchen.

"I smelled coffee and got out of bed, but when I smelled bacon, I hurried," Scott said.

Noel rushed into the kitchen. "I didn't mean to sleep in."

Sandra handed him a cup of coffee, and he hurried to the stairs.

Sandra snapped her fingers. "My mistake. I should have held off pouring his coffee, so I could talk to him." She followed him up the stairs.

Noel turned on the radio. "Did I rush out too quick?"

Sandra smiled. "No quicker than usual. When Mr. Young comes on the radio, would you let him know that we have some items to share with Lela and could use some felt if she has any."

"Message for Lela? Tom's probably on right now. I'll tell him and cut out the middle man if that's okay with you."

"That's even better, thanks."

"When will your couriers be going?" he asked.

"Right after breakfast."

"Gotcha." He put on his headset, and Sandra hurried downstairs.

She smiled at the three young boys who sat at the table when she reached the kitchen. *The boys were so quiet when they slipped past me that I didn't even hear them.*

In addition to the two girls and three boys, Scott, Cal, and Doc Larkin were sitting at the table while David and Ethan were in discussion as they stood near the utility area. David sipped on his coffee, and Ethan sipped on his milk.

Sandra fried bacon, Blanche flipped pancakes, and Louisa plated then served up pancakes and bacon. Louisa cut the small pancakes into bite-sized pieces for Aria and Jimmy before she served them.

Scott offered to cut Henry's pancake for him.

Henry shook his head. "Thanks, Papa Scott, but I got this."

Scott winked at Sandra, and she smiled. *Twenty years ago, Scott heard the same words from Stuart.*

After Henry struggled with his knife to cut his pancake he held the pancake on this plate with his knife then tore a large piece with his fork. He narrowed his eyes then side-glanced the others at the table before he quickly picked up his pancake and ripped it into slightly larger than bite-sized pieces with his hands. He picked up his napkin and wiped his hands then dabbed at his mouth. "May I have the syrup, please?"

"Excuse me," Sandra went to her bedroom, closed the door, grabbed her pillow, and laughed until the tears ran down her face. After she returned to the kitchen, Scott furrowed his brow with a quizzical look, and she shrugged. *I wouldn't have lost it if Stuart hadn't done the same thing at Henry's age.*

After Brandon and Aria, with Louisa's help, cleared the table, Scott and Blanche washed dishes while Sandra pulled aside Cal.

"Blanche and Mandy will go to the Mitchells' to take Lela some knit caps for the children to make Christmas presents for their parents. If you'll give the children their outside time after the dishes are washed, then Louisa will present this morning's lesson. The topic is weather, and specifically, precipitation."

"No surprise there. Sure, I can do that," Cal said. Sandra went upstairs with a large backpack to the storage room and quickly found the box with the knit caps. *I told Blanche fifty, but there may be more than that in this large box. I had planned to give them to the school, but the grid went down and everything changed.*

After she stopped at Stuart and Angel's room that doubled as the radio room, Noel said. "Tom said Lela had a ton of felt squares and was ready for a trade any time. When Scott's available, send him up here."

She nodded then hurried downstairs. "Where are Blanche and Mandy?" She asked.

"In the barn, waiting for you," Louisa said.

Sandra put on her warm coat then rushed to the barn. Blanche and Mandy wore warm coats, jeans, western boots, and their backpacks and carried their rifles.

Sandra handed the backpack to Blanche. "This has the knit caps for Lela."

"Good. We'll bring it back with the felt from Lela," Blanche said.

* * *

As Blanche and Mandy walked up the driveway to the road, Blanche said, "The first step of any mission is to review the rules. Our first rule is to stay together, and our second rule is to complete the mission. This might be a trick question: what is our primary goal?"

"I actually know because I heard Red and Angel talk one time. The primary goal for any mission is to return home safely."

Blanche nodded. "Exactly; what's our second goal?"

"Our second goal is to arrive at the Mitchell's safely."

"What about the knit caps?" Blanche asked.

"Is it okay to quote Angel? People are important," Mandy said.

"You're right; the knit caps are important for a project that will make people happy, and we want the project to be successful, but not if any of our people are harmed," Blanche said.

As they neared the road, Blanche said, "It's extremely important to be as quiet as possible, no talking, except if it's important for safety, then whisper. When we get to the road, we'll run. I'll set the pace because I run slower than you. A team has the slowest person set the pace, so the team can stay together. If I run to a ditch, you run to the same ditch. If I lie face down in the dirt, that's what you do. Ignore anything crawling on you or around you because we are in a dangerous situation and have to be quiet and still, no matter what."

"Be quiet; do what you do," Mandy whispered.

Blanche nodded.

When they reached the road, Blanche held out her hand for a stop, and Mandy copied her.

Blanche inhaled deeply then exhaled then took off at a fast run, but not her fastest. Mandy ran a few steps behind her.

Her instincts are good. Our profile is as narrow as possible.

As they neared the Mitchells' driveway, Blanche noticed a large transport truck on the frontage road that had slowly begun a turn onto their road, and she ran at her top speed to the Mitchell's driveway with Mandy right behind her. Blanche motioned for Mandy to run ahead of her, and when Blanche turned at the Mitchells' driveway behind Mandy, the truck completed its turn. Blanche ran halfway up the driveway then dived into the brush alongside the driveway and crouched in the thicket. Mandy was next to her and had assumed the same posture.

After the truck passed the driveway, Blanche ran to the Mitchells' house with Mandy at her side. Blanche stopped before she reached the house and put her hands on her knees to catch her breath.

"Go get Mr. Tom. I need to tell him what I saw," she gasped.

When Lela and Tom came outside, Blanche had better control of her breathing.

"Are you okay?" Lela asked as she helped Blanche to a chair on the porch.

Blanche nodded then told them about the truck, and Tom went inside. "This was the first time that Mandy has been on a mission. She did an amazing job."

Mandy gazed at the dirt as she kicked at it with her feet. "Thanks; you're a great teacher."

"Here are your knit caps." Blanche handed the backpack to Lela.

Lela peeked inside. "Goodness, gracious, this is a ton of caps. We'll be set for life. Did Sandra save any spares for herself?"

"Much more than you have," Blanche said.

Lela chuckled then put her arm around Mandy. "Come inside for a drink and a snack."

Tom returned. "Noel and Leo are on the alert. Scott and Cal are going to stay close to the road until you and Mandy return. Scott wanted to know if he should bring 48-4 to pick you up. I told Noel to tell him no, but if you'd rather he did, Noel's on standby for any changes. I'll be right back with a drink and a couple of crackers. Lela's stuffing your bag with felt."

While Blanche sipped her water and nibbled on the crackers, Tom said, "Mr. Young and I have been following the two battalions that Angel or Red named bat one and bat two. We think there's going to be a big clash tonight. Do you know about Gabe? He's a former Georgia State Trooper, and has become our intermediary for our field team. Mr. Young may have been in contact with the militia, and this is information only for our local team and can't be discussed, not even in code, on the radio at all. When Mr. Young hears there is a serious clash between bat one and bat two, he'll alert the militia, that we're calling the young boys, to attack. The last we heard the young boys were staged and waiting for more information maybe twenty or so miles from bats one and two, but this is our information from yesterday morning. There have been no updates today. Mr. Young thinks the young boys have gone into radio silence or may have made direct contact with Gabe. I'm worried, but not saying anything to Mr. Young, that something went seriously wrong."

"Thank you, Tom. I'll make sure it stays quiet," Blanche said. "Is my backpack ready to go? Mandy and I might have to crawl through the weeds and brush to get home, and I'd like to get going before I start thinking about snakes and bugs and change my mind."

Tom frowned. "I can't see that happening, but I'll support your story. Do you want me to see if Mandy's ready to go?"

"Yes, please." *I can't explain why it's urgent, but we have to move right away.*

Lela came outside with Mandy and handed Blanche the backpack. "I hope this isn't too heavy for you."

Blanche hefted the bag then slipped into the straps. "Not at all. Thanks for everything."

When Blanche strolled toward the driveway, Mandy waved then matched Blanche's steps. On the way to the road, Blanche said, "We're using a different technique to go home. Running on the road is the fastest, but right now, it might not be the safest. What could we do instead?"

"Cross the road and crawl through the grass to the trees then walk through the trees to the Newton farm."

Blanche smiled. "That's basically it. What if I'm shot and can't get up?"

"I would have to leave you and run for help, wouldn't I?"

"To quote Angel, 'Yes.' Our primary goal is to get home safely, and if the only way for me to get home safely is for you to get help, then that is exactly what you should do, but you have to keep yourself safe to do it."

"That's hard because it's completely going against rule one, stay together," Mandy sighed.

Blanche nodded. "Terrible isn't it? Sometime the Red Rule comes into play: rules are made to be broken."

Mandy giggled. "Did she really say that?"

Blanche shrugged. "Could have; she certainly follows it, doesn't she?"

Mandy nodded.

"Let's jog to the road then make sure it's clear before we run as fast as we can, which means you don't follow me, I follow you, and we dive into the grass. Ready?"

Mandy nodded, and followed Blanche as she jogged to the road. When Blanche stopped, Mandy stepped alongside her while the two of them listened then scanned the road from east to west then back again.

"Anything?" Blanche whispered, and Mandy shook her head. "Go."

Mandy raced across the road, and Blanche ran after her. Mandy dived into the grass, then Blanche joined her.

"Crawl to the woods. You lead and don't look back; trust me to meet you there," Blanche whispered.

Mandy swallowed hard then nodded and crawled toward the woods. Blanche followed her general direction but not too closely.

When Mandy reached the woods, she kept crawling until she was behind a snag. She rose and stood behind the tree.

"Well done," Blanche whispered when she joined her.

When they heard the roar of a truck engine as it sped toward the frontage road, both of them dropped face down onto the forest floor and listened as a pickup chased the first one. At the sound of shots, Blanche said, "Crawl, go."

After the shots ceased, they heard the pickup truck, then the first, larger truck headed their way.

Blanche said, "Find a safe place then freeze."

Mandy flattened herself next to a snag in the brush in the forest, and Blanche found a larger snag not far from her.

Lord, what did I get this sweet child into? We were just supposed to deliver some knit caps and bring back felt for Christmas projects.

When Blanche felt a tear slip down her cheek, she angrily brushed it away. *Toughen up, buttercup.*

Blanche furrowed her brow when she heard the large truck slowly head down the driveway that was not very far from them.

"I'll bet our security team stopped the bad guys," she whispered. "Continue with caution."

Mandy and Blanche moved quietly on foot through the woods. When they were close to the farm, Blanche motioned for Mandy to crouch while she moved closer to check the house. Scott and Cal stood next to a large transport truck, and David and Ethan trotted across the front yard from the short cut.

"Hello the house," Blanche called out.

"Come on in, honey. We stopped some bad guys," Cal said.

"Okay, Mandy, we'll go in cautiously. Stay behind me."

When they stepped out of the woods and into the clearing, Cal stared at Blanche. "You look awful. What happened to you?"

Blanche and Mandy glanced at each other then silently strode to the house.

"Angel's rule number one: sometimes there is no logical answer to an illogical question," Blanche said.

Mandy giggled.

When they went inside, Blanche handed the backpack to Sandra. "Mission accomplished, and Lela had plenty of felt to share."

"I'll put the backpack in the utility for now." Sandra said. "Mandy, the weather lesson is in the living room; you might want to join them after you brush off your clothes and wash your hands and face. Blanche, you need to do the same."

After Blanche and Mandy cleaned up, Mandy went to the living room, and Blanche hurried to the kitchen.

"Am I presentable enough for coffee now?" Blanche asked as David and Ethan came into the house.

David glanced at Blanche. "Successful mission?"

"Very, and Mandy is a very reliable team member." Blanche held her coffee cup with two hands after she sat at the table.

"We were all on alert, thanks to your warning, Blanche."

When Scott and Cal came inside, Scott asked, "What happened, David?"

"Scooter told me that when the transport truck pulled up to the house, his mother was on security upstairs at a front window. When the transport truck roared down the driveway, she yelled, 'Invaders,' and he and his dad grabbed their rifles. Phil went to the living room, and Scooter was in the kitchen. Leo came out of his radio room with his shotgun and hurried to a west window."

"Wow, even Leo has become part of their security," Scott said.

David chuckled. "I said the same thing, and Scooter told me that his wife gave Leo an ultimatum: be a security member or take care of the babies."

Scott laughed. "That Joyce is such a sweet, quiet person; who knew she is actually a bully?"

David continued, "Scooter said there was one passenger in the cab with the driver, but four men jumped out of the back of the truck. Phil slipped out the front door and lay in the tall grass in the front yard so he could hear them. Phil heard one man tell the others that they had to get the girl for Old Jitters because she knows where he is. One of the men waved his rifle and shouted, 'Send her out and nobody gets hurt; we know she's here.' While he was shouting and drawing attention, another man pulled out a flamethrower from the back of their truck and lit it then headed toward the house; Phil dropped him, and that's when the shooting started."

"That Phil is a pretty gutsy guy," Blanche said.

"Ethan and I were on our way around the house for a perimeter check when we heard the shots; I took off, and Ethan stayed with me. After we reached Leo's, there were two men on the ground, and the other four had jumped into their transport truck and were headed toward the road. Scooter ran out from the house and climbed into Phil's pickup truck; Ethan and I jumped in with him. When we reached Scott's driveway, Scott waved us down; Scooter slowed, and Scott and Cal jumped into the truck bed."

"I didn't know I married a foolhardy cowboy," Blanche said. "Did you, Sandra?"

"No, ma'am, but I guess we did."

Scott and Cal beamed.

David smiled. "When we neared the intersection, we saw the truck broadside across our road, and Scooter spun so we'd be broadside too. We had a shootout, and we're all okay, and they aren't. I don't think they were very skilled marksmen because they shot without aiming like in a movie. Scott and Cal brought the transport truck here, and Ethan and I rode back with Scooter."

"What did they mean when they said, 'We know she's here'?" Cal asked.

"Leo said they must have meant Jennie, but she had never mentioned anything about Old Jitters," David said.

Sandra raised an eyebrow at Blanche, who nodded.

"Do we know where Red is?" Blanche asked.

Cal narrowed his eyes. "She's with the field team, but we haven't heard anything in a while, have we?"

"I'm going to talk to Noel. Maybe he can get in touch with Gabe." Scott headed upstairs, and Cal followed him.

"Go away, David," Blanche said. "We've got Christmas business we'd like to take care of. Ethan, you can stay or do your project later."

"I'll go with Mr. David," Ethan said.

After they left, Sandra said, "Those two are bonding, aren't they?"

"Sure are; David's already a single parent; he could handle two boys," Blanche said. "Ready for our buckeroos? What do I do with Louisa?"

"We'll let her be support staff. I'll fill a box with a bunch of knit caps while you gather art supplies."

CHAPTER ELEVEN

Red listened as the two men argued.

"Why'd ya have to hit her so hard? Is she dead?" the first man asked.

"She was smaller than I thought; I didn't hit her head, so she has to be fine. Old Jitters would kill us if she's dead. He wants to know how she and that guy you killed found out."

They knocked the breath out of me.

"Get on the radio, but don't say nothin' about killing that cop, or you maybe killin' her," the first man said.

"Wasn't me; it was you," the other man grumbled.

"Go see if she's breathing," the first man said.

Red heard footsteps coming toward her, and she held her breath. The footsteps stopped. "This is as close as I need to get. She's dead."

Red heard a shot then a pickup truck roared away.

Red opened her eyes and without raising her head, glanced around.

The body of a man lay face down not far from her with a small red hole in his back and a growing puddle of blood seeping from underneath him.

They shot Andy. He wasn't dead when I left him; he can't be dead.

Red groaned as she pushed herself to her knees. *My shoulders hurt.* She eased off her backpack. *They broke the water bottle I'd dropped on top of my clothes, so it would be handy; my backpack is soaked, and my clothes probably are too. Wonder if they thought it was blood.*

When Red pushed herself to her feet, her head spun with the pain. *What is it Blanche says? Toughen up, buttercup; I have to find Andy. Why did they call him a cop?*

When she reached the spot where she had dragged Andy, he wasn't there; she winced at the amount of blood on the grass. *Wonder if he went back to camp?*

She opened her backpack and pulled out the sack with her snacks. She grabbed a boiled egg and took small bites. *This would be a perfect breakfast if I had a sip of water.* She dug deeper into her backpack and pulled out the small jelly jar of canned peaches. She opened the jar then drank the sweet liquid. *Ahh. I'll save the peaches for later.*

After she finished her egg, she headed back to camp; she dropped down into the grass when she heard shooting. *Sounds like a war.*

She removed her backpack then dragged it along as she crawled through the grass. *Shooting is louder.* When she neared the lane, she rested on her stomach in the grass and listened. *It's coming from the area of the battalions. Our plan worked!*

When the shooting slowed to only occasional shots then completely stopped, she smiled as she crawled in the grass along the lane Her heart sank when she saw the truck. *Andy didn't make it back to camp.*

She tried to rise to her feet, but her head spun, and she clutched for something to steady her without success. *I am so exhausted.* She dropped to her knees then to all fours and crawled to the picnic table. After she pulled herself up, she pushed then grunted as she strained to lift the table to uncover the keys. *Too weak.*

She spotted gray fabric in the grass near the spot where they had set up their tent. She crawled on all fours to investigate, then her tears blinded her. *Annie left her sleeping bag, just in case someone would need it.*

She shivered from the brisk wind as she unrolled the sleeping bag then crawled inside with her backpack. *I didn't know how cold I was.*

Red snuggled down then zipped the sleeping bag almost closed. *Andy had the radio. He must have called Gabe to come get him. I have to rest.*

She closed her eyes and sighed. *I'll move the picnic table later.*

CHAPTER TWELVE

Stuart stood next to the pickup while Angel listened intently to the radio traffic.

"Anything?" he asked.

"Nothing. Something's wrong."

"What's taking Red and Andy so long?" Annie asked. "They should have been here by now."

"They may have run into a little trouble," Jack said.

Stuart gazed at Jack, but Jack glanced away and didn't meet his gaze.

He thinks something's wrong too.

"Let's go for a walk, Jack," Stuart said.

Jack nodded, and they strode along the main street of the now deserted town.

"I think you and Annie should take the transport truck to Major's," Stuart said.

Jack's face reddened as he stopped and faced Stuart. "Why? Because Annie's fourteen?"

"No," Stuart sighed. "Annie has more than proven herself as a great team member, but the transport truck is too big to hide. Mr. Young's old white truck could be on the side of the road, and no one would see it."

"We could take the truck to Gabe's and leave it," Jack said.

"Then what do we do when we find Red and Andy?"

"Four in the back and two in the front; we've done it before." Jack jutted his jaw.

"With three of the four in the back being little kids," Stuart said. "What if they are injured and need a little extra room?"

Jack crossed his arms, and Stuart strode away.

Stubborn old man.

Stuart slowed his pace. *It's not fair to Annie to send her away; she will want to help find Red.*

When Stuart joined Jack, Jack's face had softened.

"Jack, I realized Annie would be brokenhearted if she couldn't stay and help find Red. Why don't you take the truck back to Major's by yourself?"

Jack guffawed. "No, Angel would say we have to do everything in pairs and make both of us go. We might as well leave finding Red to the experts."

Stuart furrowed his brow. "I know you're joking, but we've been trying to shelter Angel and Annie. Let's see what they think."

When Stuart and Jack returned to the white truck, Stuart said, "We need to talk."

"About time," Annie mumbled.

"Yes," Angel said.

"They should have been here by now," Jack said. "This is our meetup point. What if we leave, then they show up here? There obviously is something wrong with their radio because we haven't heard anything."

"Gabe hasn't seen them," Angel said. "I asked him about the red birds, and he told me they must have flown south because he hasn't seen any in a while."

"We need to trace their steps," Stuart said.

"Let's see if they made it back to camp," Annie said.

"What if they show up here?" Jack asked.

Annie glanced at Angel, who gazed at Annie's cloud then nodded. "Angel and I left my sleeping bag at camp in case there was a problem. We could leave them a sleeping bag or a backpack with some food."

"Mom packed crackers in an old fruitcake tin she had. We could leave food in the tin, and it would be relatively mouse proof," Stuart said.

"What about the large transport truck?" Jack asked.

"Let's take it to Gabe's. It has three large trunks with rifles and quite a few unlabeled boxes," Stuart said.

Jack shook his head. "Too much like charity; he'll balk at that. We should load some of the food into the white truck, then we can claim we took all we could."

After Stuart filled the fruitcake tin with food and snacks, he reorganized what was already in the back of the pickup to make room, then he, Jack, and Annie loaded as many boxes into the bed of the old truck as they could.

"Noel is asking for status," Angel said.

"Tell him no status," Stuart said. "Dad and Major will know exactly what that means."

"What does it mean?" Annie asked.

"It means that we have a problem but don't want to broadcast it," Jack said.

Angel slipped into the driver's seat. "Let's go."

"Annie, you've driven Mr. Young's truck; why don't you drive the transport truck and follow Angel?"

"Thank you, Dad."

As Angel pulled away, Stuart said, "Don't drive too fast; Annie's following you."

Angel accelerated as she headed toward Gabe's house.

Stuart grabbed onto his arm rest. *I managed to say exactly the wrong thing.*

When they neared Gabe's, Angel said, "Contact Gabe because he's not expecting us."

When Gabe acknowledged he was listening to the radio, Stuart said, "Angel with two chariots headed your way."

Angel slowed then stopped when she reached Gabe's driveway and motioned for Annie to pass her and take the lead into the driveway.

Jack smiled and saluted Angel and Stuart as Annie turned then drove slowly toward the house. After Annie and Angel parked their trucks, Stuart and Jack headed toward the house.

* * *

Angel climbed out of the pickup and waited for Annie, who hopped out of the large truck and hurried to join her.

Angel glanced at Annie's cloud. "How did you feel about the drive?"

"It was awesome, Angel. Dad told me that you would go slow, but you didn't, and Dad held onto the dash the entire time."

"Stuart kept a grip on the armrest," Angel said as they strolled together to the house.

Willa met them at the door. "After you all talk to Gabe, bring the men to the kitchen for a snack and hot coffee. Hot tea for you?"

"Hot tea is great for both of us," Annie said.

"It's two days until Christmas, and it's already starting to feel cold enough to snow," Willa said.

As Angel and Annie headed to Gabe's radio room, Annie whispered, "We have to find Red; she doesn't like the cold."

Angel nodded. "We'll need to wrap her with a blanket when we find her."

"Be right back," Annie said.

When Angel joined the men, Gabe removed his headset. "Did you know about the young boys? Mr. Young had contacts in the militia, and I've been their intermediary. A small militia group of men and women that we're calling the young boys staged just east of the two battalions. After you stirred up the battalions, the young boys stepped in and wiped them out."

"We have the truck that Angel and I took from one battalion, and Red and Andy signaled that they were successful in taking a truck from the other battalion, but they never arrived at our rendezvous point," Stuart said.

"They should have been there by dawn, right?"

Angel watched as Gabe's cloud turned to a protective cloud.

He's ready to go look for them.

"We need you to stay by the radio," Angel said. "They have a hand-held, but we haven't heard anything; it might be because we've been too far away from where they are."

Annie stood in the doorway of the radio room then slipped close to Angel.

"We've been using clicks on simplex to communicate," Stuart said.

"I haven't been monitoring simplex," Gabe said. "Which frequency?"

After Angel told him the frequency, Gabe set his radio to scan it. "Okay, got it. What else can I do?"

Jack smiled. "We have this little issue of too many trucks. We want to retrace their steps, but we don't want to announce our location with a big transport truck. We have Mr. Young's old white pickup."

Gabe chuckled. "An old white pickup is as common as rabbits around here. Nobody would ever notice it, so are you dumping the battalion truck here?"

"You got it," Stuart said.

They're taking too long here.

Annie elbowed Angel, and Angel nodded as Annie left the radio room.

"We have to find Red." Angel rose.

Willa and Annie came to the radio room; Annie carried a thermos.

"These good folks need to find Red, honey. I've packed up a basket for them to eat on the road," Willa said.

"You're right," Gabe said.

Willa handed the basket to Jack as they headed to the front door.

"That was awesome, honey," Stuart said as they climbed into the truck. "You and Annie were so slick that I didn't even realize what you'd done until we were almost out the door."

"I didn't either," Jack said. "How'd you do that, Annie?"

"I was feeling fidgety, so I figured Angel was too."

Angel backed out of the driveway onto the road then headed toward camp.

"Do we check to be sure their transport truck is gone?" Jack asked.

"That would be a start."

"I'll park at the camp," Angel said. "You can check the battalion one area while Annie and I stay with the pickup."

When Angel turned at the lane, she stopped. "There's a truck in the lane."

"I don't see it," Stuart said.

Angel and Annie jumped out of the pickup and disappeared into the weeds.

* * *

"I hate when she does that," Stuart grumbled as he and Jack scrambled out.

"Do we follow them?" Jack asked.

"No, there's no way we can catch them. Let's head toward the camp; if there are any bad guys, Angel will come back to tell us."

Jack nodded, and they stayed on the lane and hurried to camp.

When Stuart and Jack reached the camp, they didn't see Angel or Annie until they came out of the brush and joined them on the lane.

"We found some blood in the grass," Angel said. "I'd like to follow the trail, but we came here first."

"Show me," Stuart said.

Angel turned toward the high grass then gasped. "Annie's sleeping bag."

Stuart raced with Angel to the spot where they had set up their tent.

Angel's hands shook, so Stuart reached past her and unzipped the bag; Angel knelt next to Red and felt her face.

"She's breathing, but she's cold," Angel said. "We need to put her in the back of the truck. Spread out the blanket on the backseat, Annie."

Stuart frowned as he lifted Red from the hard, frozen ground. "Her backpack looks wet."

Angel checked Red's clothing. "Her clothes are cold but dry."

Red mumbled, "Have to find Andy because he's not a cop."

"We'll look for him after we get you into the truck," Angel said.

After Stuart placed Red in the backseat in a sitting position on the blanket, Angel and Annie wrapped the blanket around her.

"Do you think you could sip some hot tea, Red?"

"Yes, then we'll go find Andy," Red said.

"I have some tea for you." Annie held the cup and gave Red small sips.

"I'll find Andy," Angel said.

"Good," Red said.

"I told Gabe on simplex that we'd found Red, and we had one more to go," Stuart said.

"There was no blood on Red; I'll show you where we found blood on the grass," Angel said.

"I'll stay with Annie and Red," Jack said, and Stuart nodded.

Angel and Stuart crunched through the frosty weeds; after they reached the blood-soaked grass, they split up to search the area.

"Here's another patch, maybe not quite as much, though," Stuart said. "Do you think Andy's trying to get to Gabe's?"

Angel keyed her handheld. "Our other one may be headed your way."

"We'll search from here," Gabe said.

Angel and Stuart continued looking for any signs of Andy. Stuart pointed to a thick patch of weeds that was crushed flat. "Could Andy have fallen there?"

Angel examined the spot then pulled out a handheld that was half-buried in the dirt. "This is why we never heard anything more."

"Andy must have fallen and the radio was snagged in the thick weeds," Stuart said.

Angel's radio crackled. "Found your one."

"Condition?" she asked.

"Not great," Gabe responded.

Stuart and Angel raced back to the truck.

"We're returning to Gabe's," Stuart said.

"Andy?" Jack asked, and Stuart nodded.

"You drive." Angel hopped into the backseat with Annie and Red, and Jack hurried to the passenger's side and climbed in.

Stuart backed down the lane then stopped. Jack hopped out and checked the road, then motioned for Stuart to back out. Jack jumped into the passenger's seat, and before he closed the door, Stuart accelerated then raced toward Gabe's.

"I'll come too," Red said. "Annie, will you help me?"

"As soon as you warm up," Annie said.

When Stuart slammed to a stop in front of the house, one of Willa's brothers met him after Stuart, Angel, and Jack raced to the porch.

"How is he?" Stuart asked as they hurried into the house.

"Not good. He had an entrance and an exit wound, so we're sure the bullet is not embedded anywhere. We've stopped both wounds from bleeding the best we could, but Mama is afraid his shoulder might be shattered. He goes in and out of consciousness, and we think it's from the pain. Mama said he needs a doctor."

Before Angel rushed inside, Jack stopped her and Stuart. "How are we going to take Andy back?"

"If Red can ride with Jack in the transport truck, we could place Andy on the backseat of the pickup with Annie to monitor him," Stuart said.

As they went into the house, Stuart added, "I don't want to be the one to tell Red."

"Me neither," Jack said.

"Mama splinted his shoulder with cotton blankets, then we immobilized his arm with a sling and a swathe to help him be more comfortable," Willa said. "Mama gave him a few sips of her medicinal chamomile tea with white willow bark extract in it to help ease his pain and poured some of her medicinal tea into a pint jar for you to take with you on the trip. Give him a few sips on your way home to help him stay comfortable. We propped him up, and his breathing improved. He was very agitated and told us he had to find Red but settled down when we told him that Angel found her."

"If both Red and Andy can sit up, maybe Red can ride with me, and I can follow you with the transport truck," Jack said.

"Has the transport truck been emptied?" Stuart asked.

"My brothers brought in the rifles, but Mama wouldn't let them bring in the boxes because she said we were running out of storage room," Willa said. "Andy's in the first bedroom."

They followed Willa. Andy was propped up on the bed with pillows. He opened his eyes, and his smile was weak. "Is Red okay?"

"She was cold, but she's warming up. How are you doing?"

"I was cold too, then two huge linebackers found me."

"Are you up to going home? We'll prop you up on the backseat of the pickup."

"Where's Red going to ride?"

"We thought she could ride with Jack in the transport truck."

"Good luck with that." Andy leaned back and closed his eyes.

"Andy's right," Jack said. "Annie can ride with me, and Red can monitor Andy; she's going to watch his every move, anyway."

"Let's go," Angel said. "Willa gave me the jar of Andy's tea."

"My youngest brother will carry out Andy. I'll follow them and bring the pillows and the quilt. Mama said you could return them the next time you visit. Stuart, Gabe wants to talk to you."

Stuart strode into the radio room as Gabe yawned then rubbed his forehead. His eyes were sunken, and his shoulders slumped.

"Have you thought about asking for a bed in here, so you can catch a power nap while one of Willa's brothers monitors the radio for you?" Stuart asked.

"No," Gabe growled. "I don't want to be extra work."

"How often does Willa tell you to get some rest?"

"All the time; what makes you so smart?" Gabe glared at Stuart.

Stuart snorted. "I'm always doing or saying something that gets me in hot water with Angel, Red, or my mom, so I'm not smart at all, but I recognize the symptoms of an innocent man about to be in big trouble with one or two women."

Gabe chuckled. "I'll ask Willa for a bed."

Before Stuart reached the pickup truck, Annie met him. "Red told me the keys to their transport truck and its padlock are under one of the table legs of the picnic table at our camp. She wanted us to tell Gabe, so Willa's brothers could go pick it up."

Stuart ran back inside. "One more thing, Gabe." He told him about the truck at camp.

"I'll send Willa's brothers to bring it here as soon as you leave, and I'll let Mr. Young and Leo know you're on your way."

When Stuart climbed into the passenger's seat of the truck, he said, "Gabe will take care of the truck at our camp. Thanks, Red."

He glanced in the back. "Are you sitting on the floor, Red?"

"Not really; Jack and Annie put a quilt on top of a sleeping bag, so I could wrap up in the quilt to be warm and rest while I sat next to Andy."

Angel handed the pint jar to Stuart then headed south then west toward home while Annie followed her in the large transport truck.

When they were about halfway home, Red said, "Andy winced when we hit that rough patch of road."

"Angel, can you slow down a little, so I can give Andy a sip of his tea?" Stuart asked.

Angel moved to the middle of the road where the road was smoother and slowed while Stuart leaned over the seat.

"Andy, I have a little more of Mama's medicine for you," Stuart said.

Andy opened his eyes; his smile was weak as he whispered, "Good."

Red pushed herself closer to Andy, and Stuart exhaled then growled, "Sit back down, Red; you're right in the way."

"Don't give him too much at once; I don't want him to choke, but give him enough, so he'll be comfortable. You're too heavy-handed; you're going to hurt him."

While Red continued her diatribe, Andy raised slightly forward as Stuart gave him two sips of tea, then Stuart rolled his eyes. Andy's eyes crinkled as he attempted a smile, and Stuart winked. Andy leaned back and closed his eyes.

When Stuart sat back down, Angel moved back to the right lane and accelerated.

"Are you sure he's okay?" Red asked. "He looks unconscious. You need to check him, Stuart."

Angel glanced in the rearview mirror. "Hush, Red; Andy needs his rest."

Stuart held his breath then exhaled when Red mumbled, "Getting awfully bossy."

Angel nodded, and Stuart smiled.

As they neared the turn to the farms, Stuart smiled when Jack said on the radio, "Circling the nest."

Angel slowed as she passed Major's driveway, then she and Stuart lowered their windows and waved.

Stuart watched in his side mirror as Jack saluted, then Annie waved before she pulled the large truck into the driveway.

When Angel drove the pickup truck down the driveway at a snail's pace, Red grumbled, "Oh, for goodness sake, just get to the house."

Scott, Scooter, David, Sandra, and Blanche stood near the back door. When Angel stopped, they swarmed the truck. When Blanche and Sandra tried to ease Red off the floorboard, so the men could remove Andy, Red growled, "Get out of my way. I can walk into the house."

Sandra and Blanche exchanged a glance, then Blanche swooped up Red in her arms and carried the complaining young woman inside.

CHAPTER THIRTEEN

Stuart and David carefully lifted out Andy, then Scott supported Andy's legs as they headed to the house while Scooter directed their path.

"We're going to my bedroom," David said. "It's all set up."

Angel hurried in behind them. Stuart smiled when Henry squealed, "Mama Angel and Dad are home!"

Henry rushed to Angel and wrapped his arms around her. "Missed you, Mama."

Angel hugged him and kissed the top of his head. "Missed you too, Henry."

After Stuart, David, and Scott placed Andy on the newly designated hospital bed, they stood around the bed with their arms crossed.

"Shoo." Deana dismissed them as she waved them toward the door. "Scooter, Doc Larkin, and I need room to work and have no time for spectators. Tell Red I'll let her know about Andy's condition as soon as these fine doctors assess their patient."

After they were in the hallway, the three men headed toward the kitchen where Red sat at the table while she sipped a cup of hot tea and took small bites of her scrambled egg. Mandy and Aria stood on either side of her.

"Be careful, Red," Aria said. "You have to take small bites of your scrambled egg, so you don't throw up. I ate too many berries once, and I threw up purple stuff until my stomach hurt, and I cried."

"I'll be careful; I don't like to throw up either," Red said.

Sandra smiled then pointed to the living room. "Henry's showing Mama Angel his decorations on the tree."

Stuart hurried to the living room and wrapped Angel and Henry in a big hug.

"How is Uncle Andy, Dad?" Henry asked. "He looked hurt."

"He is hurt," Stuart said, "but he's got Doc Larkin and Scooter taking care of him, and he'll need some time to heal."

"Mama Sandra has lots of bandages," Henry said. "She found one for me that was a superhero, but me and Brandon decided to save it for emergencies, and Mama Sandra said we were smart."

I remember those. Stuart smiled. "Saving it for emergencies was a great idea. What have you been doing while we've been gone?"

"Secret stuff that I can't tell you because it's two days until Christmas," Henry said.

"Because it's a super-good secret, and Mama Sandra said it's okay not to tell a super-good secret," Brandon added. "You can ask Mama Sandra, but she won't tell you either."

"Pretty much shoots down any snooping, doesn't it?" David stood in the doorway as he smiled at Stuart. "Mama Sandra said if you boys would like an early supper then extra stories at story time, you should wash your hands. Ethan and Jimmy went to the woodshed for more wood for the fireplace; when they get back they'll wash then join you at the table."

Red and Scott came into the living room; Scott had his arm around Red's waist to hold her up then helped her sit down next to Angel.

"Thanks, Scott. You saved me from falling on my face and getting a big lecture from Mama Sandra or Bossy Blanche." Red smiled as he left. "So, what's up?"

"According to Henry and Brandon, only secret things because it's only two days until Christmas."

Red sighed. "That's the same story I got from Aria and Mandy. Who knew what a tight-lipped crowd we had here?" Red's eyes twinkled.

"How are you feeling?" Stuart asked as Scott remained in the doorway.

"I think I'm fine, then I try to stand up, and I realize how weak I still am; it's very annoying."

Scott cleared his throat then chuckled as he left.

Stuart smiled. *Good restraint, Dad.*

"Have you heard anything about Andy yet? I tried to talk Scott into going there before we came here, but he said he'd already been kicked out of the room once by Deana and didn't want to get banned. Can you go check for me, Stuart?" Red asked.

"Haven't heard a thing. What else did Deana tell Dad?"

Red huffed. "That she'd let me know how Andy was doing after the doctors finished examining him, but I can't imagine why they're taking so long. They must be examining him with Blanche's bug microscope, or maybe Deana forgot. Go tap on the door and ask her if she forgot to come tell me."

Stuart glanced at Angel then raised an eyebrow at Red.

"Fine; don't do me a favor." Red crossed her arms, leaned back, and pouted.

Angel nudged Stuart with her elbow, and he rose then sauntered to the kitchen.

"How about some coffee there, cowboy?" Blanche asked.

"I could use a little warm up before I see if Noel has heard anything," Stuart said.

After Blanche refilled his cup, Stuart carried his hot cup of coffee to his bedroom that doubled as the radio room.

"Anything new?" Stuart asked.

Noel smiled as he removed his headset. "Glad to see you. The militia had a very successful campaign against your two battalions and is headed east to join in the battle just west of Savannah. That campaign was a real boost to everyone and sounds like we've picked up more ground spotters. Phil, Cal, Scott, and I have planned a short reconnaissance trip south in the morning. There have been rumors of another group coming north from Florida, so we're going to check it out. Blanche called us the old time scouts."

"I might be confused, but I thought the militia was south of us."

Noel chuckled. "That was Mr. Young's mythical militia to pester your two battalions. The only news of this group from Florida has been from somewhere outside of Orlando. We don't expect to see anything, but we decided we'd like to be familiar with the area just in case we eventually need to prepare for them."

Stuart shook his head. "There's always something, isn't there?"

Before he put on his headset, Noel said, "It's how it is these days."

While Stuart was at the top of the stairway, Deana called up to him, "Where's Red?"

"In the living room." Stuart dashed down the stairs and followed Deana.

Red's eyes lit up when Deana walked in, and Deana hurried to sit next to Red, and Red clutched onto Angel's hand.

"Andy doesn't have any life-threatening injuries; he lost a lot of blood, and we have sutures and staples, but not the adequate pain medication to be able to repair the muscle damage."

Angel rose from Red's side and raced up the stairs, and Stuart followed her. When Stuart went into his bedroom, Angel sat at the radio, and Noel stood next to her.

"Let Noel know." She handed the headset back to Noel. "Jack will check the cartons in the transport truck and will let you know if we need to go there tonight."

Angel raced downstairs, and Stuart followed her. When she stopped to put on her coat, Stuart and David threw on their coats and followed her outside.

"What are we doing?" David asked as Angel raced to the white pickup truck.

Stuart shrugged. "Chasing Angel."

"We need to check the contents of these boxes for anything medical," Angel said.

"Let's carry them inside; we'll be more comfortable and won't miss anything," Stuart said.

"I'll ask Mama Sandra where we can go through the boxes." Angel rushed to the house.

Stuart and David loaded boxes into a utility cart, then Stuart pulled the cart to the back door while David loaded a second cart.

Angel met him at the door. "Take them to Blanche and Cal's bedroom."

Scott went outside to help David load the remaining boxes while Cal and Stuart carried boxes to Cal's bedroom. Blanche opened a box, then Angel went through the box and removed items, so she could examine the contents thoroughly.

"This box has medical supplies: bandages, gauze, antiseptics, and other items. I'll mark it medical, so take it down the hall to David's room." Scott left to help Cal and David bring in more cartons while Stuart began opening boxes for Angel.

"Cases of food," Angel said.

Stuart carried the box to the kitchen.

Angel quickly went from box to box and examined the contents, then Stuart handed off each box to David, Cal, or Scott and told them where the box went.

"Take this to Doc Scooter," Angel said. "It has medical supplies, but at the bottom are boxes of drugs."

Stuart handed the carton off to David, who hurried down the hall with it.

David returned. "Deana said to find more just like that because it's gold. Doc Scooter and Doc Larkin are scrubbing for surgery."

After Stuart returned from carrying a second carton filled with medications used in dental surgery, he said, "I told Noel to tell Mr. Young that we're in no rush because we're set for now."

She nodded. "This box is filled with sutures, staples, and medical equipment that looks surgical to me. Battalion two must have been planning on setting up a field hospital."

After Angel finished opening the boxes, half of them contained medical supplies, and the other half was split between canned food and blankets and clothing for cold and rainy weather.

David and Stuart carried the cases of food to the kitchen and the boxes of blankets and clothing to Sandra and Scott's bedroom, so Sandra could examine it carefully before anyone used it.

Angel peeked into the living room; Red was curled up on the sofa with Aria snuggled next to her on one side and Mandy on the other while Blanche, who sat on the brick hearth, told the story of a dragon who was afraid of snow. The three youngest boys sat at her feet, and Ethan stood guard at the doorway but was still just as enthralled by Blanche's story as the younger children.

Stuart came up behind her and wrapped his arms around her.

"It's time for us to eat dinner," he whispered.

The two of them strolled hand in hand to the kitchen. Cal, David, and Noel were already at the table.

"Louisa's listening to the radio for me," Noel said.

"She'll eat with me and Scott, then our medical team will eat as soon as they are available." Sandra dished up hot pinto bean and smoked pork soup while Scott pulled out the large cast iron skillet with cornbread from the oven then cut the cornbread into generous pieces.

He halved one of them and plated it for Angel then put the skillet in the middle of the table with a pie server, so everyone could serve themselves.

After everyone at the table ate, Stuart poured hot water that had been on the stove into the sink then added cooler water for washing the dishes. Stuart heated more water, then after Angel washed dishes, Stuart rinsed them with hot water.

Scooter hurried to the living room with Louisa at his side. Louisa helped Red to walk to the kitchen, so Scooter could talk to her while they ate.

"Red, Andy has a long recuperation time ahead of him, but he came through surgery with no problems. We'll need to keep an eye on him to be sure he doesn't have any setbacks or complications while he's healing, but Doc Larkin and I expect him to regain full use of his shoulder. The hard part for him will be to give it time to heal."

"How long will it take for his shoulder to heal?" she asked.

"At least a year unless we start him on physical therapy."

"I have a book on physical therapy exercises," Sandra said.

"We can select some exercises for Andy; he will need to keep his cardio in good shape to strengthen his core, so he doesn't train his stronger muscles to compensate for his shoulder, which happens frequently, and is the number one cause why healing an injured shoulder stalls midway. I think Blanche will be his best therapist. We'll let him have today to recover from the surgery, then Blanche can begin working with him in the morning. Mom will talk to Blanche before we leave. Now, what about you? Doc Larkin and I found some vitamins that will be perfect for you and the baby. At this stage of your pregnancy, you're the best judge of how things are going, but from a purely clinical observation, I think you and the baby are fine."

"Good because that's what I think too," Red said.

"When you're ready to leave, Doc, you have the choice of riding or walking back to Leo's house," Stuart said.

"I wouldn't mind running or walking back, but it would be easier on Mom if we rode, but don't tell her I said that because she'd be insulted."

"My mom's the same; she'd be secretly grateful but highly insulted if I suggested that she'd be better off if she rode," Stuart said.

"I'll pull 48-4 close to the house." Angel pulled on her warm sweatshirt then put on her warm jacket and gloves.

When Angel and Deana were seated in 48-4, Scooter said, "My back's bothering me from bending over so long during the surgery; care to walk with me?"

Stuart peered at him. "Sure."

As they walked along the shortcut, Scooter said, "I read the documents, and they scared the hell out me. There was a copy of an arrest warrant for Whit Ferris, and the charges included drug trafficking and racketeering; other documents showed significant amounts of amphetamine and opioid inventory shortages over several years."

"Whit Ferris? Should I know that name?" Stuart asked.

Scooter chuckled. "I got a little ahead of myself: you will; Dad told me the ham operators in Texas have been talking about troops coming through Mexico to gather in south Texas, and a few of the old timers believe an invasion is imminent. If my interpretation is correct, Ferris is a key player in the Atlanta cartel that has ties to the Mexican cartel that would have joined forces with a country that plans to invade the US from the south. He would need me to run a field hospital when the invaders moved north."

Stuart exhaled. "The supply truck that we found wouldn't be the only one headed south; how does Red fit in, do you know?"

"I think it was a case of mistaken identity. Everyone in Georgia, even Atlanta, knows about Dad and his Angel. I can't prove it, but there may have been an inadvertent leak through a ham operator who knew Leo and Angel were on the radio, and knew Dad and Leo were friends."

"Red said something when we first found her that didn't make any sense to me at the time. She said she had to go find Andy because he's not a cop, so to follow your thread, if the bad guys were looking for Angel to find you, they might assume that a young couple they found in south Georgia was Angel and her husband, the cop."

"That could be a stretch until you throw in the other gang that showed up at Leo's, and Dad heard one man tell the others that they had to get the girl for Old Jitters because she knew where he is. We interpreted that to mean that the girl they were looking for knew where Old Jitters was, but maybe we were wrong, and they were supposed to find me for Old Jitters through the girl," Scooter said.

When they reached the Smith barn, Stuart showed Scooter the well and the homestead location.

Scooter said, "I'll bet David lusts for lumber and building supplies."

Stuart smiled as they continued toward Leo's. "You got that right. He told me once that he's afraid to tell Angel because she'd bring back a truck with a load of lumber."

Scooter chuckled. "She's amazing, isn't she? It never occurred to me that I'd ever have the right equipment and supplies to perform a surgery after I left the hospital."

When they neared Leo's, Scooter said, "Now that I think about it, one of the new doctors that Ferris hired before the collapse let slip that the slight tremors in Ferris's hands were essential tremors, which is typically a relatively benign neurological condition. No one doubted the diagnosis, but Ferris was never called Jitters. If Ferris was dipping into the amphetamine inventory for personal use in addition to supplying the Atlanta cartel, the source of his shaking hands could have been from his addiction. If he graduated to meth, which is likely, his tremors and irritability would have increased. He was mean before he became addicted to meth; his men should be afraid of him."

"The pieces keep falling into place, don't they?" Stuart asked.

When they reached Leo's, 48-4 was parked near the driveway; as they went inside, Joyce said, "Angel's in the radio room with Leo and Dad, which I'm sure you already knew, Stuart."

Angel rose from her chair when Stuart and Scooter stood in the doorway.

"Let's go." Angel hurried through the kitchen and to the back door.

As Stuart followed her, he whispered, "Something's up."

Scooter followed them outside.

"The spotters reported that Old Jitters is on the move," Angel said. "A few minutes ago, Mr. Young said the sheriff wanted to host a meet and greet, and we're invited."

"I'm going too," Scooter said. "What do I need to pack?"

"Sleeping bag, warm clothes, your rifle and ammo, and lightweight snacks. Bring an empty backpack to the house, so you can load up any medical supplies you want to have along, but don't be too long because we won't wait for you," Angel said.

"Wait a minute," Stuart said. "I don't mean to be negative, but do we really need a doctor?"

"Are you running or riding back with me?" Angel asked. "Pops taught Scooter to shoot."

Scooter chuckled. "Don't know how she knows, but she's right. I'll hurry; I don't want to be left behind."

Stuart mumbled as he climbed into 48-4, "She remembers everything."

On the way to the Newtons', Stuart asked, "Why did you tell him we'd leave him if he wasn't there when we're ready?"

"Because we will."

"Is Annie going?" Stuart asked.

"I don't know, but I think Pops and David will."

"David isn't ready; he can't go," Stuart said.

When they hurried into the house, Sandra said, "Blanche took an inventory of what's in the crates and will replenish supplies. Cal and your dad will take Mr. Young's truck back to him, so their team can load up. Dad said you can use his maroon pickup truck; it's faded and almost as old as Mr. Young's, and we'll have everything ready and loaded in a few minutes. Red told me that lightweight snacks are the best and warm meals at night are important, so that's what I worked on pulling together."

"We'll need extra ammunition and rifles; Dad's pickup with the camper shell cover for the truck bed is perfect," Angel said.

When David came into the kitchen, he said, "I'll grab someone to help me put the topper on the truck."

David dropped off his backpack next to the back door. "I'm going."

Stuart frowned. "What about..."

David slammed the door as he left.

"Where's Henry?" Angel asked.

"Blanche and her cowhands are at the chicken coop," Sandra said.

Henry waved when he saw them then ran for his hugs while Brody loped along behind him.

"Aunt Red told me you were going on another trip, but it would be really short. She's sad that she can't go too, but she has to take care of Uncle Andy until he's better. Me and Brandon will help her because she gets tired."

He glanced around then motioned for them to lean closer as he whispered, "We're going to have a baby. Aunt Red told me, but we're keeping it quiet because we don't like a big fuss."

Angel kissed his forehead. "We have to leave soon."

Stuart added, "The sooner we leave, the sooner we get back."

"That's kind of what Uncle David told Brandon and Ethan. Ethan wanted to go too, but Uncle David told him it was important for him to stay and help guard the family and the house. Ethan's helping Uncle David with something now. Me and Brandon are happy Brandon's dad is feeling better."

Stuart smiled. *David covered all his bases.*

"We'll see you soon," Stuart said.

"See you sooner." Henry ran to join the group at the chicken coop.

As they hurried back to the house, Stuart said, "Henry makes me feel old sometimes."

"Yes."

After they pulled out the clothes they had worn and put fresh clothes into their backpacks, Stuart carried the backpacks downstairs while Angel and Noel talked.

"I have hot pork, carrots, and potato soup and rolls for y'all to eat before you leave," Sandra said. "If you don't have time, I'll pour large mugs of soup and give you rolls for the road."

"Pour four mugs, Mom. When Angel says it's time for us to go, we'll leave immediately."

Angel raced down the stairs as Scooter knocked on the back door then came inside.

"I'm here," Scooter said.

"We can take Dad's pickup; David and Ethan are putting on the topper for the truck bed. Everybody grab a mug of soup; we'll eat here unless everything is ready, then we'll eat on the road," Stuart said.

David came inside and picked up a mug of soup when Stuart and Scooter did.

"Noel said our spotters found Old Jitters and a band of a dozen armed men about fifty miles north of us. They are traveling with an old, open-style jeep, a troop transport truck with canvas sides, and two large enclosed transport trucks on the interstate; no one is on foot. The young boys said if the highway was closed north of Hahira on the way to Savannah, they'd be happy to join the party," Angel said.

"That doesn't make sense," Stuart said.

Sandra laughed. "If any of those Atlanta criminals were listening in, I'm sure they have no clue where Hahira is and throwing in the mention of Savannah was genius. Hahira is more in the middle of the state about twenty miles north of Valdosta and nowhere close to the east coast where Savannah is."

"That's about fifteen miles from us, using the back roads," Stuart said.

"How do we block the road?" David asked.

"With local help," Angel said.

Ethan opened the back door. "Dad, a white pickup truck is coming down the driveway real slow."

"Thanks, Ethan." David rushed outside then returned. "Jack, Major, and Annie are here."

"I changed my mind; I'm going." Red dropped her backpack next to the rest of them. "I'll take a mug of soup, and before anyone asks, Andy's okay with it; I'll even ride with bossy Annie if that's what it takes."

"What do your doctors say?"

"The usual conservative doctor stuff, but they didn't say I couldn't go."

Sandra scrambled for another tote and filled it with snacks then handed it to Red.

Scooter rolled his eyes.. "I'll ride with Major."

"Let's go." Angel finished off her soup and set her mug on the table, and Stuart, Scooter, and David followed suit. Red slung her rifle onto her shoulder then picked up her warm coat and her mug.

"Send the others in for their mugs of soup." Sandra handed Angel and Scooter the tote bags with rolls and snacks. Scooter picked up his two backpacks on his way out the door; Cal and Scott came inside then carried the crate that Sandra had refilled out to Scott's truck as Major, Jack, and Annie came inside for their mugs of soup.

David and Stuart carried out the remaining crate of ammunition and rifles and their backpacks.

Angel and Major had a quiet conversation while Major ate his soup.

After Ethan collected the empty mugs, Major announced, "I'll be on the radio with Mr. Young to coordinate our roadblock and the young boys, and Angel will lead. Load up."

As Angel headed the truck west, Stuart asked, "Are we going straight up the interstate?"

"We'll use the state roads; Mr. Young expects Old Jitters to send advance scouts on the interstate to be certain it's clear. Our roadblock will need to go into place after the scouts return for the night, then we'll put the roadblock as close to Old Jitters' camp as we dare. We'll engage them at the roadblock, then the young boys will attack from the east."

Stuart glanced back at Red then glared at her, and she met his gaze.

"Why is it okay that you are going to a roadblock that will be a shootout?" Stuart asked.

Red smiled. "Because you never go to a fight without me."

David snorted.

Can't leave out David.

Stuart narrowed his eyes. "What about you, David?"

"I didn't plan to come, but Brandon and Ethan told me I had to keep Red out of trouble," David said.

"They did not," Red growled, and Stuart chuckled.

Red glowered at Stuart. "What are our plans for tonight, Angel?"

"A ham operator outside of Hahira has a barn where we can stay. That saves us from having to set up camp or tents," Angel said.

"How are we going to find him?" David asked.

"We won't," Angel said.

Stuart furrowed his brow. "Then how will he find us?"

"He won't," Angel said.

Red snickered. "Y'all are asking the wrong questions. How do we find the ham operator's barn?"

"She'll meet us at the abandoned grocery mart on the west side of Hahira and lead us there," Angel said.

David and Stuart groaned.

"You two set us up," he said.

"Yes," Red said.

Angel held up a hand facing toward Red, and Red reached forward and smacked it.

Angel continued, "We'll leave the trucks at the barn, then while Major and Jack contact the locals about the roadblock, we'll split into three groups: one to locate Jitters and his camp and the other two to locate the scouts. When all the scouts return to camp, and our spotters say they always return before nightfall, we'll set up the roadblock with the locals about half a mile south of their camp then wait for them to move at dawn."

"Will we all be behind the roadblock?" David asked.

"No, Major and Jack will talk to the locals, then we'll finalize our positions after we gather at the barn tonight," Angel said.

CHAPTER FOURTEEN

After they neared a small community west of Hahira, Angel slowed then pulled over, and Annie parked Mr. Young's truck behind her.

Before Angel climbed out of the truck, she said, "Annie and I will walk from here. Our ham is expecting to meet with two women."

"I'll go," Red said. "We're a tighter team."

"Yes."

The two of them climbed out of the truck.

"I don't like this at all," David said.

"Neither do I. You go right, and I'll go left as soon as they get close to the grocery mart," Stuart whispered as he watched them walk away.

Angel stopped and glanced back then returned to the truck. "Stay in the truck, or you'll scare off our contact."

"How does she do that?" David asked.

"Darn clouds," Stuart said. "Wish I could edit mine sometimes."

Stuart watched as Angel and Red walked together with their heads down.

They've put together their plan.

Red slowly limped while Angel strode ahead. While Angel approached the vacant grocery mart, Red took her time and carefully watched her feet with each step then stopped and leaned against the building next to the grocery mart.

When the front door of the grocery opened, and Angel went inside, Red darted to the corner.

Angel came out of the building with a thin, gray-haired woman who wore overalls, a red-plaid heavy jacket, and a leather aviator's cap with ear flaps. Angel motioned for Red to join them, then after a short discussion, Angel and Red hurried back to Scott's faded maroon pickup.

After they jumped in, an old two-door sedan pulled out from behind the grocery mart; Angel followed it as it turned west then south onto a dirt road. The woman pointed to a lane then made a U-turn and left.

Angel maneuvered the ruts in the lane then pulled into the weeds and drove past a grove of trees. After she cleared the grove, she stopped at a large, faded barn in relatively good shape that suddenly appeared, and Annie pulled next to her and stopped.

"We're less than a mile from the interstate, but we might as well be two counties away," Stuart said as they climbed out of the trucks to inspect the barn.

"Why did she want to meet with two women, Angel?" David asked.

"She told she's been watching the groups from Atlanta, and they are all men. She said Red and I didn't look like criminals, then she asked us when Christmas was."

Red added, "I told her Thursday, and she said, 'Welcome to the militia.'"

"Let's move our stash of rifles, most of the food, and the extra sleeping bags from the back of Mr. Young's truck to Scott's," Major said. "Jack and I will have to take the white pickup to get close to Jitters, so I want minimal supplies in the back of the truck in case we lose it. Red, you're in charge of barn security; pick a partner."

"Annie," she said, and Annie beamed.

Major continued, "Our two teams to locate the scouts are Angel and David on the west side of the interstate and Stuart and Scooter on the east side. The four of you work out the most efficient way to find them all and stick with them until they return to their camp. We'll meet at the barn before it gets too dark, so we can have all hands on deck to set up the roadblock. We can't send out any search parties, so don't get caught."

Major checked the back of Mr. Young's truck and removed the last box of food, then he and Jack left.

"Do we have an idea of how far south the scouts typically go?" Stuart asked.

"According to the spotters, no more than five miles away from the planned campsite, and by now, the spotters will have a good idea of where that is," Angel said. "I'll check."

She keyed her handheld. "Did you find your horse?"

The woman who led them to the barn replied, "Took four of us, but we sure enough did. Thanks for your help."

"They'll camp about four miles north of us," Angel said.

"Do we want to follow the scouts or watch them go past us?" Scooter asked.

"Why not both?" David asked. "While one pair of us follows the scouts back to camp, the second pair watches for stragglers."

"We wouldn't have to be on opposite sides of the interstate if we do that," Angel said.

Stuart nodded. "That certainly simplifies communication and keeps our team together if we run into trouble; it was your idea, David, do you and Angel want to watch for stragglers or follow them in?"

When David glanced at Angel, Stuart did too and caught a slight wiggle of her index finger.

"We'll watch for stragglers," David said.

Stuart nodded. *Angel wants to be in a central location, so she can manage the communications, and David was smart enough to check with her.*

Stuart snorted. *Wish I was that smart.*

"Ready when you are, Stuart," Scooter said. "West side, right?"

Stuart glanced at Angel, who gave a slight nod. "Exactly," he said.

Stuart and Scooter raced down the lane and to the state road before they dashed into the woods and brush separating the frontage road and the interstate. As they quietly moved south through the trees, they kept the interstate in sight.

"Would any of the scouts be on the northbound interstate?" Scooter whispered.

"I wouldn't think so, but it wouldn't hurt to stop to make sure we're not overlooking anything on the northbound side," Stuart said.

* * *

As Major drove north on the state road, Jack peered intently at the interstate ahead of them through the trees.

"Hide," Jack said, and Major swerved the old truck across the ditch and into the brush. They jumped out of the truck and raced across the state road then crouched in the trees next to the interstate and watched as the jeep sped south with the troop truck and two transport trucks following closely behind it.

Major shook his head. "They sped by so fast, I couldn't tell if the trucks had passengers in the front seat, or if there were any passengers in the jeep."

"We know for sure they didn't see us. Do you think they have anyone bringing up the rear?" Jack asked.

"We can wait a few minutes, but I doubt it. What's your estimate for their arrival at their camp?"

"Less than thirty minutes," Jack said.

Major keyed the mic for the mobile radio. "Sunday dinner at grandma's at three thirty. Let the family know."

"Okay, Dad," Angel said.

"How will Angel know what that means?"

Major chuckled. "We agreed to have mundane communications, but the numbers are critical: three vehicles, thirty minutes; she'll know."

"Do we head back?" Jack asked.

"Might as well. I'm certain we found Jitters, and he's heading toward his camp."

On the way back to the barn, Jack asked, "Do you still expect Jitters to attack the farms?"

"Oh, yes, and I think his plan is to launch his attack tomorrow in the middle of the morning when everyone is outside working on chores; he'll slaughter the families in one farm after another, probably starting with Major's, until Scooter agrees to run his field hospital."

"What guarantee would Scooter have that after he leaves, Jitters won't murder everyone who is left?"

"None," Major said. "I think that's exactly what he plans to do."

    * * *

"Did you understand what Major meant?" David asked.

"Yes."

After six men plodded north past them with their heads down in the southbound lane of the interstate, David asked, "Do you expect any more?"

"Yes."

Angel glanced at David then gazed at his cloud. *He's processing; he'll figure it out on his own.*

"I think I get it: Old Jitters can't afford any more slip-ups; he has to have a fully functional field hospital with a talented surgeon to be able to recruit the large army he has obviously committed to delivering. It must have looked easy to him from the level of talent he sent initially, but he's got his back to the wall, and death comes with defeat."

Angel waited as his cloud brightened. "Exactly."

"What do we do now?" David asked.

"We wait for Stuart and Scooter."

When the sun slowly sank on the horizon, the air temperatures dropped as another six men slowly trudged north on the southbound lane; Angel and David ducked low in the grass. Angel maintained her aim on the man in the lead, and David aimed at the man in the rear. The last man faltered then dropped to the ground, but the other five didn't notice. After the group continued walking until they were out of sight, the last man raised to one knee and slowly crept to the northbound lane. When he reached the far edge of the interstate, he darted into the woods; Angel heard a grunt.

"Did you hear that?" David whispered. "I think we have friends nearby."

"Yes."

They waited and watched.

"I see shadowy figures," David whispered.

"Stuart and Scooter."

Angel keyed her handheld. "Red right."

"Returning," David said automatically. "That was brilliant, Angel; not many around here would understand the boating terminology of old seafarers that has long been used as a reminder that red buoys are kept to the right side when going into a port from the open sea. Major and Jack would know that we wouldn't return without Stuart and Scooter."

When Stuart and Scooter reached them, Stuart hugged Angel. "You are brilliant, darlin'."

Angel wiggled loose. "Let's go."

Angel and Stuart raced away from the interstate.

"We don't have to try to catch up with them because they'll be back in a few minutes and will run with us," David said as he and Scooter ran at a slower pace. "I gave up trying to keep up with Angel and Red ages ago, but poor Stuart keeps trying."

* * *

When Stuart and Angel then David and Scooter reached the barn, the temperatures had dropped even more. Red had wrapped her arms around her knees as she shivered even though she was bundled up in a heavy blanket. Jack stirred a large pot of soup on their kerosene burner.

Stuart crossed his arms then strode to Major. "Let's talk."

The two men strolled away from the barn. "Red has to go home; Angel and I can take her then return."

Major sighed. "I don't disagree, but let's check with Angel."

Stuart returned to the barn then put his arm around Angel and walked away from the barn. "Major and I need to talk to you."

"We need to take Red home," Angel said when they joined Major.

"How do we do that?" Stuart asked.

"I'll handle it. Does Annie want to go home with her?"

Stuart frowned.

"I'll tell her," Angel said.

Stuart and Major stepped aside as Angel strode to Annie and Red. "Red, you have to go home; we can't take care of you here."

"I'm just a little cold," Red growled. "I'll be okay."

"No, you won't," Annie said. "You've quit shivering, and you've needed me to fetch your blanket and to heat your tea. I might as well be going home too for all the good I can do here."

Stuart stared at Annie. *She went straight for the throat.*

Red's eyes widened. "I didn't ask you to do anything for me."

Annie raised her eyebrows.

"Okay, maybe a couple of things, but you don't have to go home just because I do," Red said.

"Fine; you go, and I'll stay," Annie said.

"How am I going back?" Red asked.

"Annie and I will take you," Angel said.

"Wait a..." Stuart said.

Major put his hand on Stuart's shoulder. "Careful there."

"I can't pull you away, Angel, you're too critical to the team," Red said.

"I'll go with Annie," Stuart said.

Red exhaled. "Okay, let's go."

"Are you driving?" Stuart asked.

"Oh, yes," Annie said.

"I was afraid of that," Stuart mumbled. "You drive like Angel."

"Yes," Angel said.

As Stuart supported Red when she rose, she whispered, "I hate this; I feel like I'm letting the team down."

"Red, you're making a very bold move," Stuart said. "We can absorb the loss of one team member, but we can't be effective if we're down two team members."

"You're right, but don't let it go to your head because I'll deny I ever said it."

Stuart chuckled. "Annie's waiting at the truck. I have a feeling she wants to tuck you in, so you'll be warm."

"Annie's such an old nag," Red grumbled.

Stuart held onto the arm rest and the console as Annie sped home. *She drives exactly like Angel.*

When he glanced in the back, Red was curled up with her blanket and fast asleep.

"I'm going to tell Red she snores," he said. "Will you back me up?"

Annie giggled. "No way."

Stuart keyed the mic for the mobile radio. "ETA twenty minutes; one cold; we can't linger."

"Understood," Noel replied.

When Annie reached the end of the driveway, Scott, Ethan and Blanche rushed out of the house. Blanche carried her backpack, two rifles, and her warm coat and wore her holster on her hip with her pistol.

"Is Red okay?" Scott asked.

"She's really cold. Annie and I have to rush back," Stuart said.

Ethan opened the back door, and Scott lifted out Red, then Blanche tossed in her backpack and coat and climbed in.

"I'm Red's replacement," Blanche said.

Stuart sighed in relief. "Good."

"I can walk," Red mumbled.

"That's nice; you can walk around the house all you like," Scott said as Ethan closed the door.

Annie accelerated up the driveway then headed toward the state road and the barn.

"Annie drives just like Angel," Blanche said.

Stuart gritted his teeth. "Yes."

When they arrived at the barn, Stuart climbed out first. "What a ride," he mumbled.

"We picked up a replacement for Red," Annie said as she and Blanche climbed out.

Jack said, "Glad you're here, Blanche. I've warmed up the soup, and we have hot water for tea and a fresh pot of hot coffee."

"I've already eaten, but I never turn down a cup of coffee." Blanche pulled out her tin camp cup from her backpack.

"How's Red?" Angel asked.

"Cranky," Annie said.

"Good; she's in capable hands," Major said.

While Stuart and Annie ate, Jack said, "Old Jitters had to be a passenger in the jeep. They went into the camp fast, so they were obviously expected. The transport trucks must be carrying supplies and equipment because we arrived at their camp maybe twenty minutes or so after Old Jitters, and no one had opened the back of either transport truck."

Stuart glanced at Angel as she gazed over his head. *Angel and I will take the trucks.*

Angel nodded.

Jack continued, "The locals are working on the roadblock because the camp is so noisy right now. Nothing like the enemy covering for you, is there? The locals may be finished by the time we get there. How many scouts were there?"

"There was a total of twelve in two groups. The second group must have been away from camp longer because they weren't as energetic as the first six, and the first six looked worn out. The last man in the second group feigned collapsing, then when his team didn't notice, he ran to the east side of the interstate, and we think the militia met him," David said.

"Old Jitters is making a basic mistake by running his scouts into the ground. I don't think he expects any resistance any time soon because they would probably be fine after a day's rest," Major said. "He's using the tactics for an urban gang war; if he has anyone who has military experience, he's either ignoring them, or more likely, they're afraid to say anything."

"As far as we know, is Old Jitters' plan to continue south?" David asked.

"We think so," Major said. "There's a divided highway that goes west about fifteen miles south of us."

"Whit Ferris would definitely have a preference for interstates and divided highways," Scooter said. "He grew up in Atlanta and had total disdain for what he called 'hicks.' He relied on electronics for navigation, so he wouldn't be a map reader and definitely wouldn't take advice from anyone else."

"If there isn't anything else, let's check the roadblock," Major said.

"Angel and I want to see how they've set up their camp, now that everyone is there," Stuart said.

"And Annie," Angel added.

Stuart narrowed his eyes at her. *I wish I could see her cloud.*

"David and Blanche, go with me to check the roadblock," Jack said.

"Scooter and I will take care of clean up and security for our camp," Major said. "We need to make sure we're rotating security duty, so no one gets overly tired."

"Don't be like Old Jitters?" Annie asked. "I'll keep track."

Stuart shook his head. *We have a Red Junior.*

As Jack, David, and Blanche headed toward the roadblock, Blanche said, "I'll follow your lead unless you tell me different, Jack."

"Why is Annie going too?" Stuart asked.

"Because I can't drive two trucks," Angel said.

When Annie giggled, Stuart glared at her, and she shrugged. "It's logical."

"We need to find you another mentor, Annie," Stuart said.

"Less talk." Angel ran to the state road, and Stuart and Annie raced after her. She led them through the woods and brush then paused and whispered as she pointed, "Roadblock. Hear anything?"

Stuart and Annie shook their head. Angel darted across the state road to the frontage road then into the trees and brush alongside the interstate.

Stuart and Annie followed Angel as she slipped quietly through the trees. Stuart cringed every time the leaves crunched under his feet. *Not supposed to do that.*

When Angel crouched then belly-crawled closer to the interstate, Stuart and Annie copied her. Stuart's eyes widened at the two trucks parked within a foot of them in the ditch close to the frontage road. Angel pointed to the barbed wire fence that separated the trucks in the ditch from the frontage road. Annie made a clipping motion with two fingers, and Angel nodded.

Stuart pointed south, and Angel shook her head; when he pointed north, she nodded then pointed west. *She studied the map.*

The three of them watched the unguarded trucks.

Jitters must be confident that he has his supply trucks well-guarded from any attacks from the south, but why?

When Angel darted back to the frontage road, Annie and Stuart were close behind her. When she raced across the road to the trees and brush next to the interstate, Stuart glanced at Annie then the two of them followed her as she belly-crawled to the camp.

Stuart watched as men raised a large tent then two larger tents across the interstate in the median between the south and northbound lanes; other men created lean-tos with large tarps on the sides of the trucks. A small group of men opened the back of a truck then handed out warm coats. *Why are they setting up a permanent camp?*

On the way back, Stuart said, "I didn't expect them to set up a base camp. I don't understand the strategic advantage of this location."

After they reached the barn, Major smiled. "You're missing all the fun. First Noel, then Mr. Young, and Gabe picked it up, forecasted a huge snowstorm headed this way, and it's supposed to hit us first thing in the morning. Did you see any preparations at Jitters' camp?"

"Did we ever," Annie said. "They're putting up two large tents and tarps and handing out warm coats."

"We know there is a cold front blowing in tonight, so the snowstorm fits right in; it would have been Red's idea," Angel said.

Major nodded. "She's always been our Weather Girl."

"Our bonus is that we confirmed they're monitoring the main channel." Scooter shook his head. "I suppose we may have another opportunity to cause some confusion, but it would be extremely difficult to top a major snowstorm."

"Where's our map?" Stuart asked. "When Jack, David, and Blanche return, we've got a plan to go over with everyone."

When the wind picked up, Stuart and Scooter carried the picnic table into the barn then set up the kerosene burner for hot water and coffee.

After Jack, David, and Blanche returned, Jack said, "The roadblock is great. It looks like you could crawl through it, but the locals filled it with blackberry bushes, and those thorns are wicked."

"We found the two supply trucks," Stuart said. "We didn't understand why no one was guarding them, but the impending storm must have pulled all of their resources." Stuart pointed to the map. "They are right about here: just south of the eastbound state road here. The trucks are parked in the grass, and the only thing between them and the frontage road is a barbed wire fence."

"Snip, snip," Annie said, and everyone nodded.

"When would you take the trucks?" Major asked.

"As soon as the shooting starts at the roadblock."

"Two trucks." Jack narrowed his eyes. "How are you going to take two trucks?"

Annie jutted out her jaw. "Two drivers."

"You can't be one of the drivers," Jack said.

"Really? Who else could keep up with Angel?" Annie narrowed her eyes then stormed out of the barn.

* * *

Jack glanced around the room at the disapproving faces. "Am I wrong?" he asked.

Angel put on her warm coat and picked up Annie's then left the barn.

"Good," Jack said. "Angel will talk some sense into her."

"I don't think this is going to play out quite the way you expect, Jack," Blanche said.

"What do you think, Major?"

Major snorted. "You're asking the man who barely survived raising two teen age girls, who are both headstrong in their own ways. If you can't negotiate an acceptable compromise, you're setting yourself up for a lifetime of digging in your heels and alienating your daughter."

"I'm not getting the support here that I expected," Jack grumbled.

"Yes, you are," Blanche said. "You expect your friends to tell you the truth, and they are. You're a dang good negotiator, Jack; get to work."

Jack glared at Blanche then left the barn.

Angel returned to the barn, and Stuart hugged her.

"I didn't want Annie to be cold," she said.

Stuart brushed back her hair from her face. "I know, honey. We found Red as soon as we knew she was missing. I didn't know how susceptible she would be to the cold after her hypothermia episode, but we certainly moved fast when we realized she was in trouble today."

Jack and Annie returned to the barn. "We've got it all worked out. You tell them, Annie."

"I'm really good, but I have a lot to learn, and Dad is a great trainer. Dad's going to ride with me when we take the trucks."

"Perfect team. I know I'm coming to this party a little late, but what's our plan?" Blanche asked.

"When Jitters' scouts head south, they'll come to our roadblock. We'll let them get pretty close then start shooting. We expect the rest of the camp will scramble to join the fight. The young boys, locals, and the militia will jump in and close the deal," Major said.

Jack stretched out the map on the table and pointed. "We're about here, and their camp is here, so we'll want to stage our two pickup trucks as close as possible to the roadblock."

"I'll drive Mr. Young's truck, and David, you drive Scott's; take Blanche with you, and Scooter will be with me," Major said. "As far as placement, the roadblock is filled with wild blackberry bushes, so there's no protection. We'll take our first couple of shots from behind the roadblock; David and Scooter, that will be you because you're our fastest runners. Blanche and I will be on the other side of the barrier, and we'll pick off anyone who looks like they're aiming your way. If we can draw their fire, then you can fire from the front of the roadblock. When the militia hears our fire, they'll come in from the east, so we'll need to run for the trucks to get out of there. We'll go south to the state road then head home. I don't see how it could happen, but if we get separated, we'll meet at the barn."

"How can we let you know that we have the trucks and are headed north?" Jack asked.

When Angel and Annie leaned their heads together and whispered, Stuart elbowed Jack.

"Cold chill," Annie said.

"Cold chill it is." Major scanned the group. "We're a new team; things don't always go as we planned, so we have to adjust on the fly. We have one fast rule: stay with your partner."

"Are we ready?" Jack shouted.

"Hell, yeah!" they shouted.

While everyone spread out their sleeping bags, Blanche asked, "How will we know it's time to wake up and go?"

Major smiled. "Angel won't let us oversleep."

CHAPTER FIFTEEN

"Time to move," Angel whispered, and everyone rolled up their sleeping bags and put them into the trucks.

"Do we take ours with us?" Jack whispered.

"No, we're traveling light," Stuart said.

"How do we get there? Do we ride in a pickup?" Jack asked.

"We run," Stuart said.

Jack groaned. "I can't keep up with those two."

"I can't either; they'll wait for us."

Angel and Annie raced to the door, and Stuart and Jack followed them.

When Stuart and Jack were close to their target trucks, Jack whispered, "How do we find them?"

"They'll be here in a minute or two. They heard us coming." Stuart knelt on one knee in the grass, and Jack copied him.

When Angel and Annie joined them, Angel whispered, "The trucks still have the keys in them. When the shooting starts, we'll all run to the trucks but don't close the doors until Annie and I start our engines. Stuart will signal with his handheld. I'll lead; if the headlights don't come on automatically, we're not turning them on until we're on the state road. I'll tap my brakes occasionally, so Annie will know where I am. Jack, you give the signal when we're clear. We'll be right back."

"Where did they go?" Jack whispered.

"I have no idea, and it drives me crazy, but it's worse when she disappears without a word."

Angel and Annie returned.

"We forgot to factor in Old Jitters' jeep," Angel said. "He'll take off with his driver the second the shooting starts, and his jeep is pointed this way; he'll come straight toward us."

"What are you thinking?" Stuart asked.

"Annie and Jack still grab their truck after the shooting starts. You and I shoot Old Jitters and his driver, then we chase Annie. We need to be very close to our trucks that we're stealing before any shots are fired."

"What do you think, Jack?" Stuart asked.

"It's a wild, risky move, but it makes sense, and I can't believe I'm saying that. I have one change in the details: we stick with the original plan; Annie and I will follow you."

Stuart furrowed his brow. *There's a chance Jitters may have three or four men who are assigned to guard him. It would be difficult for Angel and me to stop five or six men before we were shot.* He glanced at Angel, who stared over Jack's head.

"Yes."

"Major gave me heavy duty wire cutters; while Angel checked out the jeep and the troop truck, I cut the barbed wire where Major told me, so we're set," Annie said.

"What did you do to the jeep and troop truck?" Stuart asked.

"Tossed the keys under the jeep; Mr. Young can let the young boys know where they are."

* * *

After Angel, Stuart, Annie, and Jack left, Major asked, "Do you think you can drive without headlights?"

"I don't see why not," David said.

"Ready when you are," Blanche said as she hopped into Scott's pickup.

Major headed to the frontage road and David followed him.

"What do you know about the militia, Major?" Scooter asked.

"They're an all-volunteer group, but they are dedicated to keeping their families and others safe. They were small, disorganized groups at first, but they've come together and grown as the threats increased. Their leaders are experienced military officers, and most of their troops are young men and women who were military veterans, law enforcement officers, or skilled craftsmen. Why?"

"I've got the supplies and the skills for a field hospital, my family is safe with Dad and Mom and the people at the Newton farm, and I can return to my calling of saving lives. I'm questioning my motives, though; it is really worth leaving my family for the excitement of being a part of an army defending its country?"

"Sounds like you've been thinking about this for a while," Major said.

"I have. I decided not to join the militia until after I was certain my family and parents were safe at Leo's. The truckload of field hospital supplies that Angel lifted was a bonus and took away any concerns I had about having supplies or equipment. Now, my only concern is whether I can cut it."

"I won't give you any advice because you don't need it, but if this is a consultation for a second opinion, you'll be an asset to your unit," Major said.

Scooter chuckled, "Thanks, Major. I appreciate the support."

Major slowed the truck when he neared the roadblock. "Right side of the road looks better to me to park. We won't be hidden, but we'll be out of here not long after daybreak."

When Major pulled into the shallow ditch, David followed him.

After both pickups were parked, everyone climbed out with their rifles then quietly closed their doors.

Major glanced at the dark blue sky with the sliver of orange on the horizon. *The scouts should be at the roadblock any minute.*

The four of them hurried to the roadblock then waited.

A man shouted, "The road's blocked. That big tree near the road must have been hit by some big downburst last night."

Another man called out, "You're waking up the whole camp; just go past it and quit complaining."

As more men gathered near the roadblock, Major whispered, "At your discretion."

David and Scooter ran to the far end of the roadblock together; both of them fired two shots then raced back and stopped to fire two more shots each. Blanche and Major stepped out from behind the trees and fired into the confused crowd who were rushing toward the roadblock with rifles or scrambling to get away from the roadblock. David and Scooter took several more shots from the front of the roadblock, then Major called, "Go."

As Blanche turned to leave, she grunted then fell to the ground, and blood soaked her jeans from her left upper thigh to her knee.

She pushed herself up on one elbow then motioned with her other hand. "Just go on."

Scooter knelt next to her and examined her wound. "Two-man carry."

Major stepped between Blanche and the interstate and fired repeatedly.

David swept his arms under her armpits and lifted as Scooter lifted her legs.

"Stay low," Blanche said as they raced with her to Mr. Young's truck. Major continued to monitor the interstate behind them as he followed them.

"I need a little time to examine her wound. Can we go to the barn, Major?" Scooter asked.

"I'll follow you, Major," David said.

The two pickup trucks roared away and headed toward the barn.

By the time Major reached the barn, Scooter had cut away the jeans from Blanche's left leg and dressed then wrapped her wound. Major jumped out of the pickup and pulled out Blanche's sleeping bag from the truck bed.

"This is going to be cold at first, Blanche," Major threw the sleeping bag over her.

"Brr," she said. "Understatement of the year."

"I've stopped the bleeding, but the bullet is still in your thigh, Blanche. My preference is to rush home where I'll have a more sterile environment, more equipment, and more appropriate medications than what I brought, which means I learned that I need to rethink my field pack."

"I'm happy to help; let's go," she said.

"I'm sure he knows, but I'll tell David to follow us."

When Major climbed out of his truck, David met him. "How's Blanche?"

"She's stable; Doc Scooter stopped the bleeding and wants to take her home to treat her wound properly."

"I'll be right behind you." David dashed to his truck and followed the old white pickup.

* * *

While it was still dark, Angel, Stuart, Jack, and Annie crept to their target transport trucks then stood behind them. At first light, Angel elbowed Stuart, then he heard shouting from the roadblock.

No shots yet. What's taking them so long? Did they have a problem along the way?

Stuart exhaled when he heard the first two shots and scanned the camp.   *They*   *aren't*   *reacting*   *very*
q   *u*   *i*   *c*   *k*   -
ly.

After more shots, a man with a rifle ran to the tent closest to the jeep, then trotted out carrying a large backpack. A second man followed him with a rifle and a warm jacket.

"Ready when you are," Stuart whispered, and the two men dropped to the ground almost simultaneously.

Stuart scanned the camp. *No one is coming this way.* "Go," he said, and all four of them jumped into their trucks.

Angel accelerated after she crossed the ditch and headed north.

"Cold chill," Jack said on the radio.

"We made a mistake," Angel said. "We didn't set up a response to cold chill, so we'd know when the other team was clear."

Stuart furrowed his brow then spoke into his handheld. "Chilling status?"

He turned up his volume and listened for a response. David said, "Red right."

"Returning," Angel said. "They're on their way to the barn."

"Let's go."

Angel continued north for a few more miles until she came to the road going west. Before she turned, Major said on the radio, "Clear sailing ahead."

Stuart frowned. "I don't know whether that means they've left the barn, or we should go home. What do we do? Go home?"

"Yes."

When the sky darkened, and a light mist became heavier, Angel said, "This rain looks funny. Is it because the truck's wiper blades are old?"

Stuart squinted at the windshield. "Turn off the wipers." He chuckled. "You can turn them back on; it's Blanche's snow. Didn't you see snow in Cincinnati?"

"I remember the flakes being big and fat when I watched them from our apartment windows as they fell, then the piles of snow on the streets were gray."

Stuart nodded. "I don't think we'll see any big flakes or piles of snow, but it will still be exciting, and I don't think any of the kids have seen snow, so they'll be ecstatic."

"We didn't get Henry anything for Christmas."

"I'm sure Mom and Dad have covered for us and for David."

Angel peered at the road then slowed down. "I checked the tires, and they are good on both trucks, but I don't know this truck, Annie doesn't know hers, and neither of us has driven on slippery snow. I'll go a little slower."

Stuart exhaled. "I know Jack will appreciate it."

"We'll take the trucks to the Smith barn. There aren't any padlocks on either truck, so we could do a quick survey of the contents then run home."

"We can take Jack and Annie home with 48-4 if we beat the pickups home."

When she turned onto the road that led to the farms, Angel said, "I'm so glad it's still snowing. Do you think it will snow all day?"

"That's a Blanche or a Red question," he said.

Annie followed Angel down the Smith driveway, and Scott and Cal waited for them near the barn.

"So, what did you pick up this time?" Scott asked after Angel and Annie parked their trucks.

"We don't really know yet." Stuart opened the back of his truck and hopped into the back, and Jack opened his and climbed inside.

"They're packed full, aren't they?" Scott peered into the backs of both trucks.

Stuart moved boxes around as he read the labels. "I have more medical equipment and supplies and three large olive green tents. This looks like another supply truck for a field hospital and the personnel." Stuart shifted boxes, so he could see the boxes that were close to the cab. "These are marked coats, pants, and boots."

"I have about the same," Jack said. "I did find several boxes that are probably food."

"We brought 48-4 to give you a ride back to my house in case you and Annie are anxious to get home. All your things are in Mr. Young's pickup, so it's ready to go. Quick update for you: Blanche was shot in the thigh, and Doc Scooter is removing the bullet. Deana said Blanche will be fine after a little recuperation time if Blanche will cooperate. I think Sandra's got a plan," Scott said.

"Ready to go?" Cal asked as Jack and Major closed the truck doors.

"I'm grateful I don't have to run," Jack said.

After the four of them left, Angel locked both trucks then put the keys into her pocket and picked up her backpack and her rifle.

"Your pace," she said.

As they ran, Angel held out her hand and giggled as the flakes hit her hand then melted.

When they went into the house, Henry squealed, "Mama, Dad! Dad said he'd make sure you were home for Christmas. Did you see the snow? Ranger Blanche said it would snow. This is the best Christmas in my entire life."

Angel hugged him, then Stuart wrapped both of them in his arms.

"Did you know Ranger Blanche was shot? She's a real hero. Doc Scooter took out the bullet, and Dad told us that Ranger Blanche has to take it easy, but she'll have more time to tell stories," Brandon said.

Red came into the kitchen and rushed to hug Angel.

"Come see Andy; he's already complaining about being stuck off alone. Doc Scooter gave him permission to sit in a wheelchair for a bit after he rests. Mama Sandra said we'd have hot chocolate and cookies after the kids go outside, then after supper I thought we could sing a few Christmas songs. Stuart, your mom found your guitar that you'd put away, and Scott and Cal picked up mine from Pops' house as a surprise. I had completely forgotten about it; I didn't bring it with me when we left Florida because we were only coming for a quick visit, but Aunt Molly brought it with her."

Red led them to Blanche and Cal's bedroom. "Andy and I were in David's room, and David was upstairs in our room, then when Blanche came in, David's room became the surgery suite again, so she and Cal will be there until she's well enough for us to switch rooms. Scott told me that Mama Sandra lived for the bedroom shuffles, and I believe it."

"How did it go?" Andy asked when they walked into the room.

"We shot two men who were running toward a jeep, and the young boys took care of everyone else," Angel said.

"How many trucks did you steal?" Andy's eyes twinkled.

"Two, and Annie drove one home. We have the equipment and supplies for at least two field hospitals and clothing and food for the staff," Stuart said.

"I don't have a lot of energy yet, but I'm not going to miss out on the hot chocolate." Andy closed his eyes.

"How's he doing?" Stuart asked as he strolled back to the kitchen with Angel and Red.

Red smiled. "He's doing fine, but he's not going to heal as fast as he expects."

When they reached the kitchen, all the children wore snowpants, mittens, and warm coats with the hoods tied under their chins. Brody and Tracker made the rounds as they sniffed each child.

"There you are, Angel. We're going to make snow angels for you. Wrap up warm!" Louisa said.

Mandy smiled. "We're excited it's Christmas Eve."

"I am too," Angel said.

"Red, Mama Sandra said you could watch from the kitchen window. I'll wave to you," Aria said.

"I've never made snow angels before," Henry said. "Did you, Mama?"

"I never did; I'll grab my coat and go outside with you."

As they went out the back door, Sandra pulled out a batch of sugar cookies from the oven and slid in the next batch.

Angel and Stuart watched as the children made snow angels then rolled in the thin covering of snow; Brody and Tracker raced around the yard then dashed to the back door. Brody scratched, and Red opened the back door for them.

"Smart dogs," Stuart said.

When Scott came outside, he asked, "Anybody ready for hot chocolate?"

Everyone trooped inside, and Sandra and Louisa helped the children remove their wet snow clothes then hung the damp garments to dry near the stove. Scott, David, and Ethan hurried to Blanche's room to help Andy into the wheelchair.

Sandra and Louisa poured the cooled hot chocolate into cups with lids, then everyone except the medical team went into the living room. Noel came downstairs with a handheld and joined the group.

Red and Stuart tuned their guitars while Mama Sandra handed out two cookies to each child.

"I have a fresh pot of coffee to go with the cookies, if anyone is interested," Sandra said. Scott, Cal, and Noel went to the kitchen then returned with cups of steaming coffee and a handful of cookies.

After everyone was settled, Red and Stuart took turns selecting Christmas songs, and the adults joined in. Louisa sang harmony to Red's clear, soprano voice, and Noel's bass tones added depth to Stuart's baritone. Stuart smiled as he scanned the young, joyful faces as the children listened to the adults sing.

After five songs, Red said, "I have to rest; maybe we can sing more songs this evening before bedtime."

"How about a Christmas story?" Stuart asked.

"Christmas story?" David said. "I'm your man. Did I ever tell you about the Christmas bear?"

All the children shook their heads.

"Once a young bear decided he didn't want to hibernate," David said.

"That means sleep during the winter in his cave," Brandon said.

"That's right." David continued his story. "Because he wanted to see what Christmas was all about."

Stuart hugged Angel and whispered, "This is why we had to be back before Christmas."

Angel kissed him. "Yes."

Sandra motioned for Scott, Stuart, and Louisa to join her in the kitchen, and Angel followed them.

"I need a little Christmas Eve consultation, and my planning partner got herself shot. We used to always have grilled cheese and tomato soup on Christmas Eve. I think we need a Christmas Eve tradition. What do you think?"

"We have goat cheese and crackers; what do you think about chili and beans?" Scott asked.

"I'd forgotten about all the chili and beans that Molly and I canned the last time Annie harvested a deer," Sandra said.

"Biscuits and chili," Stuart said. "Goat cheese and crackers are our snack."

"I love to make tortillas," Louisa said. "Wouldn't that be a treat with chili?"

"Chili and tortillas is perfect; now, what do we want to do about Christmas morning breakfast?"

"We used to always have cinnamon rolls," Scott said.

"Remember when we used to have cinnamon-sugar toast, Mom?" Stuart asked. "Why not cinnamon-sugar biscuits?"

"That sounds good," Louisa said.

"I'll add scrambled eggs and bacon, so Red will get extra protein, but I won't be singling her out," Sandra said. "Next item: do we open presents before or after breakfast?"

"That's a hard one," Scott said. "I think feed everybody as they get up then open presents after everyone eats."

"What do we do with the excited children after they eat?" Sandra asked.

Angel dashed out of the kitchen and down the hallway.

"Where'd she go?" Louisa asked.

Stuart smiled. "No telling."

Angel returned. "Woody has boxes of children's books in his bedroom; he suggested that Louisa go through them and pick out a book for each child, and David find a book for Ethan to read."

Scott gazed out the window, "I think it's snowing a little harder. Has our wet gear dried yet?"

"It's wearable. Are you thinking about going outside?"

"If you don't mind sacrificing a few cardboard boxes, I think we can slide down our bit of a hill in the front field."

"I'll pick out the books as fast as I can because that sounds like fun," Louisa said.

"We'll help you," Stuart said.

When the children came out of the living room, they were talking about the Christmas bear.

"Anybody interesting in wrapping up and going outside to see if we can slide down our hill?" Scott asked.

Henry, Brandon, and Jimmy headed toward the backdoor, and Scott said, "Whoa there, pardners. Mama Sandra will help you put on your snow gear."

After all the children were dressed for the snow, Scott led his parade of children who carried flat, oversized boxes outside.

After Louisa, Stuart, and Angel picked out books, they carried them downstairs to the kitchen table.

"Am I released?" Louisa asked.

"Go ahead," Sandra said. "I've cut out bookmarks for the children to decorate, except I'm calling them seat cards because they will stay at each child's seat until tomorrow morning."

"Shall I relief Noel, so he can go with you?" Angel asked.

"He'd love it."

Angel and Stuart went to their bedroom. "Dad took the children for sledding, and Louisa plans to join in the fun. Would you like to go with her?"

Noel gazed out the window. "It's snowing harder. Thanks, I would."

As he rushed out of the room, Angel put on the headset, and Stuart hurried to Red and Woody's room then returned with a book and settled down in his overstuffed chair.

Stuart was deep into his story when Angel said, "A Christmas baby."

He put down his book. "What?"

"Charo had a baby girl a half hour ago, and everybody's excited. Tom said mother and baby are fine; Charo and Nate named the baby Christina and will call her Chrissy."

"I'll run tell Red," Stuart said.

Angel nodded then turned her attention back to the radio.

After Stuart returned and settled down with his book, Cal came into the radio room. "Henry would like for you two to watch him slide down the hill; I'll take over radio duty."

Angel and Stuart hurriedly dressed for the snow then went outside with their rifles.

Stuart handed his rifle to Angel. "Hold my rifle for a second." He swept up snow with both hands and tried to form a ball then threw a flurry of snow at Angel.

She giggled. "Did you just challenge me to a snowball fight? Here, you hold the rifles." She swept up some snow and tossed it at him with both hands.

Stuart laughed as the soft snow blew around him. "We either need more practice or more snow."

Angel took back her rifle then he held her hand as they hurried to the front field.

Henry stood at the top of the small incline that was being called the hill. He waved. "Watch me."

Henry sat on his cardboard then Brandon pushed him on the hill, and Henry began his slow downward descent. When he stopped, he picked up his cardboard and ran the rest of the way.

"Did you see how good I can ride my sled? I have to go back; it's Brandon's turn."

Henry trudged up the hill then gave the cardboard to Brandon, who sat on it then nodded. Henry pushed Brandon, and Brandon slid down the hill then stopped.

"These children will sleep tonight after all," Stuart said. "I was afraid Henry would be up half the night from being excited about Christmas."

"Dad's a genius," Angel added.

They stayed to watch for a while, then Angel said, "It's too cold to just stand here; let's go inside."

When they went into the house, Sandra said, "Good, somebody came in, so I don't have to go out there to tell them it's getting dark, and supper's ready."

They raced to the top of the hill.

Stuart said, "This has to be the last time down the hill. Mama Sandra said that supper's ready."

Brandon sat on the cardboard box, then Henry pushed him to the bottom of the hill, and the other children did the same.

"What do we do with the cardboard, Dad?" Stuart asked.

"Leave them all by the back door, and I'll run them out to the garden for weed control."

After Stuart, Angel, and all the children were inside, Stuart and Angel helped the children take off their snow clothes then sent them to wash for supper.

Sandra scooped up chili into bowls while Louisa put a plate of medium-sized tortillas in the middle of the table then showed the children how to roll them.

While the children ate, Scott, Noel, and David came inside.

"It hasn't slowed down a bit," Scott said. "We might get an inch or two of snow after all."

While the children ate, Sandra said, "We'll have a new routine tonight. After everyone eats, and the dishes are done, we'll have bath, songs, and stories with snacks then bedtime."

After the adults ate, Brandon, Henry, and Jimmy cleared the dishes then Aria pulled out the chairs, so Mandy could sweep under the table.

When the dishes were done, Louisa took the girls upstairs for their baths, and Noel and David took the younger boys to the downstairs bathroom for their baths.

"I love that we don't have to haul or heat water for baths, thanks to our well and water heater solar systems that Angel put into place for us," Sandra said.

"It's especially appreciated with all the kids we have in the house," Scott added.

While everyone gathered in the living room, Stuart and Red planned their songs. Stuart strummed a few chords and Red joined in, then they sang the first song. Red raised her eyebrows at Louisa, who elbowed Noel, and the two of them joined in. Sandra gave the children sugar cookies to munch on while they listened.

After five songs, Red leaned against the sofa to remain standing.

Stuart said, "Let's close with a Red solo." He strummed the opening chords, and Red smiled then sang 'Silent Night'.

When the song ended, everyone was quiet for a few moments while the memory of Red's voice lingered in the room, then they burst into applause and cheers.

"I have a short story about a family who was looking for a place to stay one cold Christmas Eve," Scott said.

Stuart helped Red to Andy's room, and Angel followed them.

"Your voice is beautiful, sweetheart," Andy said. "I could hear you very clearly."

Red kissed him lightly. "Thank you, I was hoping you could hear me."

Stuart and Angel left the room.

"I'd like to do our perimeter check after we tuck in Henry," Stuart said.

When the children filed out of the living room, Stuart and Angel took Henry by the hand and held on as he hopped from one step to the next. Henry lay down on his bed and yawned. "Tomorrow's Christmas."

Goodnight," Stuart said.

Angel kissed his forehead. "Sweet dreams."

As they walked around the house followed by Brody and Tracker, Angel said, "The wind and snow have already filled in all the footprints in the yard."

When they were halfway around the house, the dogs abandoned them.

"Dogs went back inside, let's hurry, so we can too," Stuart said.

After they went inside, they went to their room, and Angel took over the radio while Stuart read by kerosene light until his eyes were too tired to read.

"Let's go to bed." Stuart extinguished the lantern.

CHAPTER SIXTEEN

Stuart woke and peered at the sky when Angel elbowed him. *The sky's a little lighter.*

"Do you hear that?" she asked.

Stuart listened then he heard Henry mumble, "Be quiet, Mama. He might hear you."

"Sounds like he's dreaming; I'll go settle him down," Stuart said.

Angel nodded and sat at the radio.

When he returned he asked, "Are you coming to bed?"

"Tom was on the radio; the young boys reported the jeep was gone when they went to pick it up, but they found the keys to the troop truck."

"How could that be?" Stuart asked. "We killed Jitters, and you removed the keys."

"Maybe we didn't kill Jitters. Somebody took the jeep before the young boys got to it; I think Jitters took it and followed us. I think he's at the Smith barn waiting for first light."

They quickly dressed then tiptoed downstairs.

"Mom's already up," Angel whispered halfway down.

When they went into the kitchen, Cal sat with Sandra. "I'm too restless to sleep, so I got up when I heard your mother making coffee."

"Could you take over the radio?" Stuart asked. "We want to check the transport trucks."

"Sure." Cal refilled his cup then tiptoed up the stairs.

"Have some coffee." Sandra poured a cup for Stewart. "Do you want some hot tea, Angel?"

"Later," she said.

"I'll take a cup of coffee." David hurried into the kitchen. "I heard you get up, so I got up too. What are we doing?"

"We're going to check the transport trucks," Stuart said.

"Good idea." David grabbed his warm coat and put it on. "Ready when you are."

After the three of them left the house, David asked, "What's really going on?"

"The young boys didn't find the jeep. If anyone followed us, they'd be at the Smith barn waiting for daylight to kidnap Grayson."

"What's the plan?"

Stuart stopped and looked at Angel.

"We make noise at the trucks to draw Jitters out of the barn," she said.

"I can open up the back of the truck that is farther from the barn and ask Doc if he's seen what's in the truck," David said.

"Here's the keys. Separate set for the two trucks," Angel said.

"If I'm positioned at the truck closer to the barn, I should have a clear shot when he looks out," Stuart said. "Where will you be, Angel?"

"I'll be at the back window of the barn in case he decides to come out behind the trucks."

"Do we think he's alone?" David asked.

"We don't know," Angel said, then she disappeared.

David frowned. "Do we wait here?"

Stuart sighed then nodded.

Angel returned. "The jeep is parked near the trucks in the brush. This time the keys are in my pocket."

When they reached the Smith barn, Angel and Stuart took their positions as David hurried toward the farthest truck from the barn to open the back.

"Wrong keys," David said. "Give me a second, and I'll have this open for you, Doc."

After David opened the back of the truck, Stuart aimed at the man who crept out of the barn with his rifle raised to shoot. Stuart fired once. David picked up his rifle and aimed it at the barn, but no one else came out.

"Clear," Angel called from inside the barn.

Stuart shook his head. *She went through the window to check the barn thoroughly. Why does she do stuff like that?*

Angel joined him, and spoke to Leo on their alternate simplex channel. "Need Scooter at the Smith barn for ID. No field bag required."

After Scooter identified the man as Whit Ferris, also known as Jitters, David said, "I'll grab Scott later this morning, and we'll take care of the body."

When Angel, Stuart, and David returned to the house, Henry, Brandon, Jimmy, and Ethan were sitting at the table eating breakfast.

"Happy Christmas," Henry said. "After we eat, Jimmy's mom has a surprise for us."

"Me and Mandy planned what we'd wear on Christmas Day," Aria said as she and Mandy came to the table in Christmas shirts.

After the children ate, Louisa said, "Remember the bookmarks we made yesterday? We have books for you to read while the adults eat breakfast, and when they are finished, you can mark your places with your new bookmarks."

Louisa handed each child the book that she and Stuart had selected for them. As soon as Henry, Brandon, and Jimmy had their books, they dashed to the living room to read.

After all the adults ate, Sandra said, "We'll do the dishes later; let's open presents."

David and Noel left the kitchen then rolled Andy in his wheel chair to the living room. Red tucked the blanket around Andy's legs before she sat in the chair next to him.

Cal and David pushed Blanche's bed down the hall, so she could listen.

Scott read the tags then gave each present to Louise, who handed them out.

"For Henry from Mama and Dad," Scott said.

When Henry opened it, he hugged Stuart and Angel. "I love my tractor, thank you."

"That was my favorite tractor when I was your age," Stuart said.

"It's my favorite tractor too," Henry said.

"Next is for Brandon from Dad," Scott said.

When Brandon opened his present, he laughed. "This is a nice block of wood, Dad. What are we going to carve?"

"Whatever you decide," David said.

"Ethan, your present isn't under the tree; we'll take it outside later to see how it works for you. Do you want it to be a surprise, or shall I tell you what it is?" David asked.

Ethan's eyes were wide. "What is it?"

"A deer rifle. You're old enough to help feed the family."

Ethan hugged David. "Thanks, Dad."

Angel and Stuart opened their presents from Henry. Angel's cap had a hand-drawn angel on the felt, and Stuart's cap had a man holding a rifle who wore a cape. Angel and Stuart put on their knit caps and beamed.

"These are perfect Henry, thank you," Stuart said.

"They're the best, thank you," Angel said.

Henry giggled then sat with Brandon and Jimmy.

Stuart put his arm around Angel while they sat on the sofa and watched everyone open presents; he whispered, "This is what Christmas is all about."

She lightly touched his face then snuggled against him. "Yes."

ACKNOWLEDGMENTS

Huge thanks to my husband for his patience, support, technical expertise, and guidance. Every day is adventure and finds a spot in a novel, doesn't it?

Thanks to my faithful family, friends, and talented editor for their support and encouragement!

Thank you for reading! *You keep reading; I'll keep writing!*

Tell a friend how much you loved Season of Danger and a leave a short review with your favorite bookseller. Authors can always use a few sparkles to brighten the gloomiest days.

PRO TIP: Post a five-star rating or recommend a book: both count the same as reviews!

Ready for news about what's next? Subscribe to my not-your-typical newsletter. https://judithabarrett.com/newsletter

ABOUT THE AUTHOR

Judith A. Barrett, award-winning author, lives in rural Georgia on a farm with her husband, two dogs, and a dozen chickens. She writes post-apocalyptic science fiction, thriller, and cozy mystery novels.

When she's not busy writing, Judith is busy with farm chores, walking with her husband and dogs, or watching the beautiful sunsets from her porch.

Website   www.judithabarrett.com

Newsletter   *Subscribe* to her eNewsletter via her Website